CW00518649

His Invisible Hold

His Invisible Hold, Volume 1

Tanya Coleby

Published by Tanya Coleby, 2023.

HIS INVISIBLE HOLD.
BOOK ONE

Written by Tanya Coleby – ©2023

Cover by brosedesignz-bookcovers.com

I wanted to be a mermaid or if not then a unicorn. Sadly, I could not be either one of those, so I became an author instead.

DEDICATION

To those who could not be here and who are sadly no longer with us - such as my eldest big brother Tim.

I often lay awake wondering what is out there in the afterwards. I guess one day I will potentially find out what it is.

Could it even be invisible vampires...

TRIGGER WARNINGS

This book contains mention of suicide and past assault both physical and sexual, but it is not graphic in any way or gone into in that much detail and the attackers do get their comeuppance eventually!

It also contains mild spice and violence that some readers may find disturbing.

Or even interesting perhaps...

His Invisible Hold.

Then

As he forced himself through the bright lightening and the glorious rain that had hit the town from out of nowhere, Iden finally reached the location that he needed to desperately be in right then, and he carefully squatted down onto his polished booted heels steadily and then waited impatiently with firmly crossed arms for a sign to proceed.

For patience was not his game; impatience was his second name as he liked to say to anyone that would listen to his important words.

He as he had stopped, folded his magnificent black wings down with relative ease and moved them so that they retracted into his slightly muscular body at the back and then, so they were no longer in the way of what needed to be done.

They were so darn big, huge, so perfect though in every way apart from that, that he only used them for mere flight, his soul journeys also, and then to accept that he had to get rid of them for a time. Even though it smarted to do so sometimes if he kept on doing it.

Flicking and un-flicking his awesome wings back in and out of his back to move through the flock.

But where would he really be without them as a part of him?

He had a job to do there that needed to be done.

That was it. The time was then.

Without them he would be stuck on only two pointless feet instead of wings, and un moving much like the mere humans who lived down below him currently were. A bit pointless of them really even though he himself used to be one, many moons ago.

As he stood holding onto his two usual glowing remarkable swords, gripping one tightly in each hand for defence - his own chosen personal weapons that were meant for him. Because they might be needed that day if the moment so struck him.

Possibly something else instead.

He did not know yet, but he had an inkling.

For someone out there was at the brink of death; he felt their life's energy wither away from them until it was almost non-existent and unnoticeable by any others around them, and it were now seemingly ready to leave the world for pastures new and judgement that were yet undecided.

He could sense it.

He could smell it so sharply as it went from a fruity wholesome smell that he wouldn't mind sinking his sharp teeth into, to devour in every way possible with every fibre of his being, to a then beyond bitter smelling one that got to the senses straight away, filled them with repulsiveness, and he would only devour their crimson blood if he were totally desperate to do so.

The soul out there would not hold on for much longer, he could feel it changing as he sought it out, so he needed to be quick with this and find them fast.

To help them.

Because wasn't that what he was made to do? To help. To carry. To protect.

Not knowing the age of the soul or their situation that they were in he would have to wait till he reached it to find out any more.

It was always a surprise to him. It always would be but that were the buzz of it for him.

Sometimes when he were feeling bored and had nothing else to do right then, he would play stupid guessing games about which souls that it would be that day that he had to deliver to the judgement gate by a certain time on a certain day.

The gate that seemingly had all the answers to all the questions that no one else did so. The one he had to go to multiple times per day that he could go there when blind folded and still find it easily and without any delay at all.

Because as one of the gate keeper Vampires, it was his job to take the recently deceased souls off to one of the four realms that were there in existence on planet earth.

The human world not included in this.

Realm one was for one's judgement, the judgement realm.

For it was not usually the gate keeper vampires place to decide the persons last fate and whereabouts, and about whether the soul embarked onto lower or even higher plains but a higher being beside, that even he did not knew of who that were.

Or they.

He had never seen them.

He had never over the years caught a glancing sight of them or heard their name mentioned from others quick and loose gossiping lips.

Once he had arrived to the judgement realm with the soul clutched tightly in his arms then and only there it would be decided which of two other realms available that the awaiting soul would be soon taken to whilst he departed back to his own home.

Alone. And soul free.

Realm two – the higher realm for those deemed to be worthy of being there for all of eternity, the good included, or realm three - the lower one. This was the one that nobody wanted to get into ever if they could help it as it was for those deemed unworthy.

The bad. Criminals, liars, cheaters and all else similar and in between.

The ones that most people were glad that they had died or felt no to little sorrow. No one missed them or else they had done terribly bad things and committed ghastly crimes for one to speak of.

Realm four – his own dream home that he loved more than anything else in the realms – the hidden vampire realm. This was located high in the blue skies above not far from realm one, three was much higher up then them and his own one could only be seen by those people that participated in a mainly blood only diet – the vamps.

Hidden from the humans. It was not for their eyes to see.

Humans only knew about two of the realms – they knew of them in their dictated versions as heaven and hell. They did not know of otherwise to this.

They never would until death became them, then their every wish would come true – or else their everyday nightmare would be unveiled to them.

As he paused in breath for what next awaited him, a figure landed not too far away from him. A shadow that loomed.

He spun round hastily to see who dared to encroach on his own space, his own territory at an important time like this one. It had better be important or else, he seethed inside as he felt the other male shut their wings down, ready to talk he guessed!

His own purple tinted blood, the blood colour of the vamps like he, boiled madly inside.

He gritted his fanged teeth, now unamused by his being joined by another. In the realm, in his clan he was surrounded daily by his own various people. Here was supposed to be about solidarity.

It had been the way for thousands of years. He was nearly as old as time.

His dark blue, slightly tinged black eyes glowered at the threat in some kind of dark and dangerous warning. Whoever it were would now know not to mess with him while he was this way. He let out a small, fanged growl that showed his dislike.

The figure spoke to him as it neared.

"Oh, I`m sorry Iden, I had no idea that you were making this trip! I felt the call here after my last one, there was a fear that the call would not be answered as it took so long to be answered." A strong masculine voice said to him in his usual hoity toity tone that implied that he really wasn't that sorry at all by him being there also.

His words a dig at his leader. But they were still friends.

Sort of.

It was only Barren, another gate keeper that he knew well.

A friend if you liked to say - perhaps. He normally worked nights as his preference, so they did not often clash.

He would recognise that posh voice that grated his every nerve anywhere. Barren was also dark haired, but it were slightly lighter than his own, lean, he was well to do, had been brought up with money whenever he needed it, a private boarding school and – he shouldn't be there with him.

Not right then. Not ever.

Iden`s eyes flipped to his and they shone so very bright.

"No, I was nearby, Barren. I could sense the anguish all the way from over the way."

His friend nodded to him in silent stilled agreement. The smell that they could sense was unnerving, even for two as old and hardened as they were.

A younger vamp would have faltered at the unpleasant stench that first hit them on arrival and would likely struggled with the smell of bad doings. Because badness was here.

Barren made a wry face, "Me too. I will leave you to do with this yourself then as I know you are more than capable of doing."

"That is true."

"Plus, it smells... no, it`s not for me. There is badness here that can only pull you down into the deep unknown. Be safe Iden. I`m off now. Good luck!

Barren shuddered openly and sniffed again and with a sudden flap of his own miraculous wings he was soon off out away into the crest of the huge spinning world. Back to where needed him for it wouldn't be long.

Back to where called his name.

Iden got back to the task in hand of taking the poor soul to where it needed to soon be. He flew off in a hurry at the speed of light and searched around the small Norfolk town which were not far from the main city, where he felt its presence, with his brilliant eager eyes until he at last saw the crumpled, broken figure of a petite built, small female surrounded on the floor by four dubious males, who after obviously doing somethings so horribly disgusting, so vile to ever be able to comprehend, that words would not come to him right then, they thankfully ran off into the darkness hopefully to crawl back where they came from.

It did not matter one iota to Iden though what they now did.

He was a bit of a homing beacon his clan liked to say; they could run from him - these people, but oh dear god they would not hide from him on this world and this world alone.

Maybe any. Not that they would have the pleasure of inheriting wings like his when they hurried up and died a gruesome and painful death.

Nor did they for a moment deserve to.

Once he had knocked them down, stolen their crimson blood that ran through them like a river. There would be little left to take. Their flesh left for the wolves and the wolves alone or left for the morgue to dissect.

He had done far worse over his many years if he were so honest about it.

The downer earth when he visited it to him was mainly full of nice, decent, law-abiding people. But there were also those there that did frankly despicable things to their own people that made one shudder with disgust and ill ease.

A bit like his own realm really, sure, but they were in the minority there in his lands.

He hurriedly reached the beaten tiny woman within moments of spotting her limp and deflated on the ground. At first sight he thought that she was merely a child as she was so small, barely five foot tall and no curves to call her own.

If that had been the case, then all of his realm combined could not have prevented his brutal, explosive wraith that he would have inflicted on her attackers. But she was an adult. Still not good by any means, still not right what they had done to her in any way but at least dear god better than that idea of it having been done to a mere defenceless child.

Every fibre of his being wanted to hot foot it out of there though, out of this becoming over whelming situation and to chase the grotesque, hideous men down.

To make them pay for what they all did to her.

To wipe them from existence forever and to torture them until the years passed on and nobody even remembered their names.

Or wanted to. Because if they did then he would torture them too.

But he feared that this woman here on the floor like a pretty discarded doll, needed him right now.

He knew it. He had earned it...

He would be gravely punished by those higher up the chain then him if he left her to go off to fight justice with those scummy supposed men. Leaving her to die alone was not the right thing to do.

But it was what he currently wanted to do.

He cautiously without touching her frightened soul sat down next to the strong but small, needing help woman. He covered her with her torn clothing to protect her modesty and then cradled her head with his large, warm hands.

Power emitted from them to calm her. To bring her peace.

Now placing his own weapons down next to his side in case they were needed in the near future. But right now, the threat had gone and passed. It was just him and the souls owner.

"Who, whose there? Have they gone now?"

The precious brown-haired woman asked him fearfully through unshed tears lining her lashes that he wished so fucking hard that he could remove with a simple lone finger, but he already knew she was already sensitive from her recent fearful struggle with her unashamed attackers.

To touch her right then could be her undoing.

But it was ok, soon she would feel no fear at all, no pain at all, where she was going to be going once her last breath on earth were finally drawn.

Well... not unless that were that she ended up placed into the hell like lower realm, but he strongly, strongly doubted it.

"Yes, young one. I will not hurt you so do not fear me. Please."

He nodded earnestly.

Young to him, for he was all eternal and mighty and would never likely permanently die unless someone tried to off him like they had tried before. But he were stronger than most, only the hand of his brother, his elder brother, could be the one that ended him and his clan leadership for good. Only being in his early twenties when he had perished the human world and then became whole again, but it were now many, many moons after as he were a vamp and in a never- ending cycle.

He had lost count somewhere along the way quite how long it had actually been since he had left his home far down on earth.

He did not know why he had nodded to her in his reply, why he did this anyway as she could not even see him at all with her own innocent eyes.

Just a habit of his maybe? He nodded to his clan, he nodded to the souls bearer.

She to his surprise spoke in a wee, frightened voice, a hint of a Norfolk accent entwined in it. He was well aware of the area for it was one of his favourites, "I can't believe that...I can't believe that just happened. I was just walking home from my dear friend Cindy's and then these men appeared out of nowhere and then they..." This was said In a confused harsh whisper that he only just heard as he had enhanced hearing. "I asked them to stop...but they never did." She gasped at the pain of it all.

He cringed at her shaken words. "I am a friend, a friend when you are in need. I am going to touch your hand, hold your head if need be young thing, but I swear down to the almighty god above that I will not touch anything else of you without your consent. I promise."

Unfortunately, he had been here before too many times for his own non- beating heart to cope with.

"Ok... I can live with that." She muttered unsurely.

So, he reached down to her carefully and touched her hand which he gripped with his own larger one that encased hers. Magically he let his miraculous essence pour out - this would give her a bit more time to be able to speak her last words to him, for he felt that they were needed to be heard. They needed to be spoken. They were – important.

To give her consent to what he was about to ask of her. Because that was the important thing.

"Shh young one, you do not have to explain further anymore to me." He said this, his eyes going red like blood in pure anger at what he had just witnessed even just a mere glimpse enraged him.

Outrage was an understatement.

His stomach was strong but for a moment it had simply weakened.

He was not angry at her. Not at her- never. For she had done nothing wrong here.

At them.

He had seen many bad, dark things in his time as a soul collector and prior to that even what with having a bad brother, but that act was the lowest that humans could possibly get to. Even the majority of the darkness, the lost ones that he knew of in his own realm would not step that far out.

It was an act that only monsters wielded.

"Who are you?" she asked him in confusion with no ounce of fear on her pretty face. A groan that shot through his core. "I... I can't see you..." She started humming nervously which seemingly seemed to help her to relax somewhat.

She could not see him, no, not yet but she would be able to feel him though, smell him. Touch him. For he was invisible not lifeless.

He sighed, wondering if she even wanted to see him.

Always hating this part right about now.

It had went round and round again multiple times that he had had this same conversation over the years with the soul he had then come for.

Why did they even make vampires, the gate bringers invisible, he often cursed silently to himself? Yes, the humans would not see them at all, but in his view surely those at their last breaths and then on after they deserved to see who was taking them to the beyond rather than them being unknown to them and simply being unseen?

"I am taking you to your final destination." He uttered proudly of the fact that he was, it were he and he alone.

She gasped before he could say anything further to that. Realising that, that meant she had come to a final end. She were dying. She had seen the film final destination. Those words could only mean something bad.

A soul collector would only be sent when the persons death was inevitable. When the kiss of life, chest compressions and the help of machines would fail to work and could not bring the human back to life.

Animals had their own path to take in which they did not deal with. The animal entered a paradise of its own for purely animals much like the upper realm. For there was no bad animals, only bad owners. That were unless the animal wanted to be with their owner again if they had passed to the upper realm.

If their owner was instead placed in the lower realm, then the pets could not go there with them. For it was not them being punished, it was not their fault that there owner had done unspeakable things. They would be looked after or else be free and their owner would suffer for their mistakes alone.

Back on the floor the petite brunette woman trembled as he spoke of her final destination, "Where is that?" She whispered.

"A better place then here." He answered.

For it was. There was no better place to be, and he could vouch for that.

The girl let out a small but stifled sob, "I do not deserve a better place then here. Am I going to... am I going to hell?" She was nearing the end of her life there. Her breath was often more shallower. Every so often she let out a sharp gasp from where her ribs had sunk in her small chest.

But it was inevitable either way.

This way or that there was no turning back now that she reached this far into the unpleasant near end of her life.

Even with the extra boost from his magical hands that he had given her, he had to hurry, he had to do this now. He had to finish this off once and for all.

He simply must.

Or else he would live to regret it for all of time. He did not know what, he did not know why, but something drew him to her. A major pull that he could not go as far as to explain to anyone without appearing chronically insane. She must feel it too if he did as well.

She had to live on. She must.

Well kind of...

"Never!" He snapped crossly at her but then regretted it as she flinched. "We call that the lower plain, Hell like I mean. If you are sent there, then I will eat my own wings for you are not going there."

She chuckled though through pain, despite herself.

Despite what she had been through that thankless evening alone. Despite that she would not be going through anything again on the earth and she now knew it as each breath hurt more and more to make. Each breath drew less air then the last one had. Soon there would be no more.

That were scary stuff. To wonder if each rise and fall of her chest would actually be her last one taken there.

It did not help that her ribs hurt so very much, everything hurt from all the merciless kicking that had been inflicted on her poor small body when she had laid out cold on the ground. And at their cruel mercy.

This sudden chuckle from her brought a smile to his thin but impressive lips. He beamed for a time then grew solemn again as he remembered his place.

His eyes went from red to a fierce bluey- black as he relaxed for a moment into himself, like the situation was becoming much more under his control.

He knew what was coming, "You have wings? I bet they are so beautiful." She said this in a soft murmur, either to him or to herself. "I wish that I could see them. I wish that it were the last thing that I could see. There is nothing else I could possibly want now that everything else has been taken from me in this world."

For she were fading fast.

Soon it would be her goodbye to this world.

"They are." He smiled warmly. Knowing that they would be firm friends. "You will."

She frowned, "Are you an angel? Is that why I cannot see you?"

"Pah, don't insult me young one." He grimaced internally at this, and he could sense her tense up, go rigid, as she realised that he was insulted by his sharp tone and being called an angel. So, he said, "No, I am less angel but more else besides that."

"That does not make much sense. Does it?"

How could she not understand him he wondered?

"Well to me it did." He sniped back cattily. For it had when he thought about it.

He had always been proud of his spectacular, black wings that graced his back body, angel or not. For angels did not exist in the way humans thought that they did. If they did then everything everywhere would only be filled with goodness.

"No, I will take you to the judgement realm, which is where all the lost souls go to, and then they will take it from there. Not to worry, please, please don`t. I have been through this so many times before and it is pretty much fail safe. It has to be."

He could not bear that if she worried, even if she had compared him to the stuff of mere legends. What else did she believe in?

Devils?

Preposterous! There was a god he assumed. But a god that they would never see.

"That is a relief." She sighed on learning that she was going to be ok. Kind of.

He decided to just come out with it, to tell her his unexpected offer before she ceased to exist.

For soon he would be needed for another soul to take elsewhere. It was often back-to-back with little time for sweet relief in the in-between of realms.

Would she accept it? Even if she became someone like him? The majority did who he had asked previously. Few said no to it, but then again few got asked to by him.

The realms needed balance.

He bit the bullet and asked what were on his mind, "Now then... I don't often do this but here goes- a proposition for you lass - I can give you another option here young one besides the judgement realm, an alternative to it if you like. I am a vampire soul collector, not an angel at all. My name is known as Iden Fortheart, leader of the Fortheart clan. I can if you consent turn you into a vampire too much like me, and like my own people are. You can join me in the vampire realm for all of eternity, platonically, and we can come back to earth whenever you so desire, or you can even stay here as long as you can take souls to the judgement realm when so needed and on time.

"Oh." She hesitated but was listening to him eagerly.

"We drink blood, there is that one thing that you might find a flaw I do have to admit, although it is tasty once you are urm... changed...but..."

A beyond evil smile went onto his curved lips and his black – blue eyes glowed magnificently red again in his moment of unashamed malice. "But you can take revenge on those vicious men who dared do that to little ol you. One who I gathered was just a sweet innocent but sadly is one no longer due to them. The revenge will be yours and yours alone to do with as you wish...if you choose to do so that is. If not, I will take you onto the judgement realm with no quarrels at all besides."

He hoped she was keeping up with all this. That it would make sense sometime soon in the near future.

He remembered his own time when the choice had whirled around and around in his handsome head for a time. Although in the end he hadn't been given one. He said let me think about it, but he didn't really want to live anymore then, and they had changed him anyway.

Now he must live on forever. His punishment for what he had done.

The trouble was that the clock was ticking on, and the decision would be almost permanent.

She did not hesitate or take her time like he thought that she would do even for a mere moment, a cold look on her simply perfect face was placed there instead.

"Yes."

"Are you sure about that?" He said this in a husky cool voice. He could not turn her into a vamp unless she so wanted him to do so.

For he himself, hand on cold heart, was a peaceful gate bringer. And not one of the darkness who would turn the unwilling without their consent like had been done to him. They did not care as long as they made more like them. More to be under their control.

If anyone blew their cover it would likely be a member of the darkness or three.

But he were instead proudly one of the good clans.

These darkness vamps who did whatever the heck they liked, when they liked, and they only got away with it as they did the bare minimum and did what they were told sometimes, to earn their unfound freedom and the lack of punishment for their crimes.

Their preposterous ways. Their not playing by the rules. He thought that most should have been annihilated.

She nodded swiftly.

Seemingly nervous but also excited at what was to come.

"Say it again."

He hissed this sharply, then caught himself as he realised that she had tensed up again and was pulling back from him. He was too eager to succeed, so he were doing this somewhat badly.

His mouth actually watered in earnest at what he soon sensed would happen for him.

His dinner was nigh, and he could smell it already, taste it with his imagination. He needed the blood high and soon it would go more sour.

He needed it to fly.

"Yes. Turn me into a vampire like you and I can then make them pay. I will make them all pay!" She said this with a shocking cackle like a wild witch as she tilted her head back.

He almost expected a black cat to appear from behind them.

And a pot brewing with potions.

A brief explanation first at what he must do to help her transform, "First I will bite you, drink from you, and then after I have had my much-needed satisfaction you will drink my powerful own blood to start the transformation into - the undead."

"Wow..."

"Wow? Is that fine then?"

"That is fine." She did not look too sure now and were frowning with small brows, but she had already agreed with him and so in his mind eye there would be no going back now. The blood lust was starting to hit him full speed. He could not stop it even if he wanted to when it took over.

"Ok. Then we will begin then. Once you are at the start of being a baby vamp, you will be able to see me." His fangs soon sprung free, making his mouth look sharp and him appearing almost deadly, if he weren't hidden from ones sight. He gently pulled her head away from his lap and he found her slender neck, looking for the perfect spot to feast upon.

"Oh, that tickles." She said rather nervously as she felt his hungry breath search for a drink to call its own.

"Hmm." He was now to busy thinking of his next meal to speak. The vampire in him was at the front and the man hidden at the back.

Her. His next meal. She smelled like rare steak a smell that he wanted to try so darn much.

The blood that was pumping through her veins he could not wait to have down his throat.

Then he hastily bit down with his fangs. She yelped out in shock, not from pain no, as he were surprisingly to her relief - gentle, but he continued on sucking her blood up and into his awaiting mouth.

Oh, she was perfect, he thought as he was now in somewhat of a blood daze! High on the feeling, it would never get old to him.

She tasted just simply... wow.

After a few minutes, maybe ten of glugging on her gently he at last finished devouring her. The feeling was almost erotic but the only sexual relief he would get during the vamp- turning act would be with another.

With her...

He then quickly bit down into his right arm and held the cursed blood, his blood, what she needed to transform, in place over her awaiting small dainty mouth.

"Now drink my blood young one, and you will be like me. You will see me and all the other vamps once that is done. I promise you this. I will never lie to you."

He roared like a titan.

A roar that would be heard for miles. But the source of it only seen by her.

"Yes, yes I would like that!" she cried out also as she opened her mouth and awaited in awe for what was to come.

It was kinda awkward as she could not see him in any way, only feel him with his fingers reached out to steady her head. He smelt like a day at the beach when she was a little girl playing with her sister in the sand.

Salty, sandy, fresh. wholesome, she bet he looked good with it.

How could he be not? But now she did not care of his appearance. She would be given another chance at life; she would no longer feel weak and defenceless.

She would no longer be someone's victim. They could be hers.

She drunk his blood with her eyes closed hard and hoped that none would spill.

To her it tasted - a bit weird, and it was also strangely intimate to guzzle him down with her lips. But she still drunk it anyway, to get her where she wanted to be.

She had to.

It was either that or to be dead - dead. Well, she would be kinda dead anyway either way no matter what happened here on in!

As she felt him remove his arm from her open mouth, she opened them brightly. She could see all the more clearer now.

"I...I can see you." She gasped now in shock at the vision before her. Disbelief.

To her he was indeed truly and remarkably handsome and definitely unworldly, there was no other explanation for how exquisite he were. She could feel the goodness coursing off of him and she knew that this man, this vamp whatever he were- was her saviour.

For that she would ever be thankful of. She could never repay him no matter how hard she would try over the years to.

"Good." He ran his fingers gently through her now messed up hair and she shuddered in response to his amazing touch that made her want to croon. "Only by my people and in the realms, I can be seen, not down here and also there is possibly only one human on earth who can see me. She may also be in my realm of the undead although that is... doubtful. But I have not met her, nor I fear I ever will." He lowered his head in a brief moment of sadness and met her eyes with a sorrow filled to the brim.

So, she were not the only one filled with longing and loneliness right then. She could not believe that a creature as divine as him would ever feel that way.

The brunette felt sorrow. But not her own, "That is quite sad if I am honest. Can I ask who is she? My name is Ruby by the way." She held out a hand in polite greeting.

The name quite suited her he thought in wonder. He knew they would be firm friends eventually.

He had a sense about people.

Although his soul was not as pure as it should have been, for he rarely gave his blood to anyone no longer for it were his and he had been maddened in the past by events that had passed there course.

But she, she had deserved another chance at life.

A chance to get her ultimate revenge on those terrible, arse wipes.

He held out a large hand and smiled and swept it along her without touching her again. Her clothes changed swiftly into brand new ones, for he knew that she would not care for her old, soiled ones that were torn on the ground in a heap next to her.

A modest blouse and trousers, that would do for now until she chose her own ones.

Of that she would have plenty.

Her pain was now gone, she were now fully healed.

Physically at least. Mentally... that might take her a while.

"It is time."

If he took much longer, he would be in danger of not being available for another souls fair end and that would not do.

He picked her up into his toned arms, for her wings would not be ready quite to break free on her back as of yet.

Maybe a day or so to flourish and she would be off, off, up and away.

Often a month it could take in rarer cases.

As he held her in his arms and made to fly away from her place of death, she stared at him.

She now saw him.

For she was after all being carried by a tall, handsome, dark headed stranger with a truly lean figure and muscles like he went to the gym on the regular. But she knew without a shadow of a doubt that he was nothing like the evil men from before that had brutally attacked her on her way home and had left her to die alone in pain.

The only fear she now held was at what would await her in the vampire realm when she arrived in his arms.

What would it be like?

Would they like her there? Could she do this fearsome task of taking souls onwards and upwards to this judgement realm that he spoke of? Well... now she guessed that she had to as she had agreed to it. It would be her job to in exchange for... well this. Being a vampire.

He was silent for a brief moment and only spoke as they neared the judgement realm high in the sparkling sky. The one that she would not have seen before as she were not a blood feaster, it would have remained a mystery to her.

Iden gently said, "You asked of the one that could see me. Who will see me. My mate. We all have a mate. I am invisible to every mortal, every mortal except for her....my human mate.

CHAPTER ONE

N^{ow} <u>ELFINA</u>

Elfina leant over the already heavily tattooed, larger than life man and got to work on what he had not long asked for her to do for him in her shop. He had requested a vibrant tattoo on his upper arm in memory of his dearly beloved mum, who had recently passed away due to her heart finally failing after many years of reluctant heart issues.

Now it was his that were truly broken.

She would give him what he wanted that day with a sincere professional smile on her red painted mouth, and she would aim to do it as well as could be.

She was well known for the pieces that she created in her own shop in a city in Norfolk.

The city of Norwich.

The one that she had fought tooth and nail for to call her own, but that now belonged to her without any debts hanging over her pretty head. Used with the proceeds of her uncaring parents estate when they had made a ghastly end.

Not that they ever liked her. It was like they had never wanted children. Why did they have them?

She did not know. She didn't want to take their money. But this shop for sale had called her name. And it was a final fuck you to them after all the years of misery. To use her parents own money on something that they would have hated.

She might not have got her dream otherwise.

She carried on with her marvellous creating needles, in firm concentration on the man's upper arm until the piece was then finished, after a few hours of slogging with little to no rest for her.

She did not care how long it took. She would do as he wished.

The man once the piece were finished, hoisted himself up from the blue chair once she had covered it for him for hygiene reasons, and once she had gone through the aftercare regime with him so he could look after it once back home.

For you would be surprised what some people put on their tats once they returned to their homes!

"Thank you so much." The man welled up with emotion at it.

She were glad that he liked it.

The older man now was obviously moved to tears at the memory of his dear departed ma that were now forever in place on his arm in her memory.

She herself had no tattoos in memorial of those that she had lost. Though there was only one for which she had cared enough to mark her skin in that way.

Her sister.

In her view it would hurt too much to see their name etched on her for all of time. She already thought about them each day. The pain would not go away.

But she understood why some would like that reminder of the fallen ones to be on their person.

She could then feel herself welling up as well at the sight of the emotion pouring out of him with no shame to it. Nor should there be any.

She had no one herself though left to live for.

No family.

Just no one at all. She had lost everybody dear to her in her whole world except her few friends that had stuck by her through thick and thin, and she knew the pain that he felt like it were her very own, as she went home each day only to be greeted by her awesome dog Sniggles and no husband or kids to speak of.

No patter of feet or genes passed down.

No mum or dad to ring up and chat with. Hers had been awful that she tried to shake the memory from her mind.

The pain that one day her customer would actually hopefully begin to overcome and break free of, but that there would still be a piece that he carried around with him day by day throughout his entire life.

A painful but freeing reminder of a mother who deserved to be remembered.

Unlike her narcissistic one.

"That is my pleasure." She beamed this radiantly at him and smiled dearly, looking at his thick slightly hairy arm that now wielded her own proud mark on it, that made her happiness soar.

A mark that this gentleman, a man in his sixties, would carry until his death, which she hoped was far away from that place in time.

Lately she had been thinking about what happened after it all happened.

Was there anything out there in the beyond? A heaven, a hell, or something in between maybe? She was not religious in any way, no, not really. But of late it had been bugging her about what was out that when she finally closed her eyes and entered her eternal sleep.

Something that had only increased as her sad thoughts grew.

She saw the man politely out of the shop whilst idle chit chatting as was her way, and then put the closed sign over the door with a sigh.

It had been relatively quiet that were for sure, but she were still glad to finish for the day. She went out into the small entrance hall between the flat and shop and trod up the steep carpeted stairs to her own flat.

The bonus of having a flat right above her own shop was that she could be there for her cute and cuddly jack Russell whenever she had a free gap in customers, and she could then let him out for cuddles and wees.

She swiftly unlocked it then pushed the door to with a start whilst peering round cautiously, for you could never be too careful about who may jump out. Her beautiful dog ran over to greet her from whatever escapades it had then been up to in her absence.

"Sniggles!" She yelled happily in greeting to her favourite four-legged friend ever as he ran over on four small paws. She knew that if her dog could talk back to her that he would have replied with his own enthusiastic words of encouragement in response to her warm greeting to it. Instead, her loyal dog just stuck out its short tongue likely after being up to some form of mischief (probably eating something) and wagged its stumpy tail in merriment to its favourite person coming back to him.

"Let's go get some food boy."

She said with a loving pat.

As her stomach churned loudly also in protest at her apparent hunger from not having had the time to have eaten much that day, she needed it very soon.

Oh, she had eaten something light, for it would not have been the done thing to actually faint whilst tattooing a customer, but not enough for her build to actually survive on.

Her dog seemed to nod in reply to her as he were always hungry, he could never get enough, but she must have dreamt it though.

Dogs didn't nod!

She fed her little Sniggles and herself something that she rustled up for them both and then wandered back over to the main bedroom aimlessly looking around it in tired, zombie like mode.

There was two bedrooms in her flat, one that she used to sleep in of course and one that was so full of her clutter that she needed to sort it out before it became unhabitable for guests.

In which there were few.

She then to her surprise heard the door flap go with a sharp clatter and then the sound of footsteps disappearing, which put her on sudden edge. The dog as well, as he yapped.

On high alert.

She frowned, wondering what it could be.

And who.

She must have left the downstairs door leading to outside unlocked for them to even be able to reach the letter box to her flat! Luckily the shop had its own other entrance.

Oh no! She reached the letterbox swiftly in a tread of feet with butterflies in her curvy stomach that would not ease until she knew what it were that had come through her door.

Her own personal sanctuary.

Hopefully just a takeaway leaflet or one of those weight watchers ones that came a bit too much. Nothing to fuss about. Nothing to get antsy about! She tried to remain calm.

"Oh no!"

But she knew as soon as she saw it what it were in there, sticking out where it had not fallen onto the hall carpet.

It was from him.

It could only be from him; he was back, he had found her, and he must know where she lived now! The around about year gap in correspondence from him had been a red herring that had made her think she had heard the last of him.

For good.

Was there no getting away from him? Was this her life from now on in? This wouldn't do.

He couldn't have her. She wouldn't give in to him. She wasn't his, she was waiting for someone else.

She felt anger like nothing before hit her full stream with an almost imploding rage and she could have screamed aloud like a mad banshee if she didn't have next door neighbours to think of

A yummy bakery- handy that smelt amazing, and a butchers the other size that smelt -gross.

She was settled there now finally.

A shop, flat, a cute dog, and living near her small group of friends. Why couldn't he fuck off and die she asked herself?

She didn't like the thought of being alone when he had been so near, so eerily close, and so grabbed her mobile phone off the side quickly in a clammy hand and dialled someone who she knew could help her right then.

They couldn't eradicate the problem no, not unless they had a gun and wasn't afraid to use it, but she could not ask her friend to serve jail time for that stalking prick so they could instead lend a caring ear when she needed it the most.

Like then.

She knew she was off work.

"Lovella?" She asked shakily to her friend as they finally answered the phone.

Lovella, she would know what to do she always did within reason. She would be there for her; she could guarantee it.

"Hello my lovely." She heard her friends sweet melodic voice ring out over the phone speaker and she breathed a sweet sigh of relief with it that she were now not alone. Working alone and living alone could be a lonely state of existence at times that not everyone understood.

She released her held in breath in a puff of air as she spoke in a whisper.

"He's back." She said simply for her friend would know who she meant with no further explanation to it. There was no need to say who she actually meant because they all knew who had been plaguing her.

Who would not let up in constantly nudging his way into her life.

The others had regretted the actual day that they had introduced her to him in a casual manner at a party that had turned into a lingering, kind of warped obsession with her, that no matter of everyone trying to solve it, it hadn't seemed to have reached a conclusion.

"Oh no! Are you sure it`s him?" Her friend asked stupidly. For there would be no other that would rear his watching head just when she thought her life was back on track.

Brief silence.

But then -.

"Positive."

"Wanker."

"Mmm. Can you come over? Bring the crew if you can do. I cannot face ringing anyone else about this and my heart is whirling sitting here alone with just the dog who would likely just lick him to death if he broke in here and tried to..."

The dog gave her a seemingly nasty look on hearing that dig aimed at him.

The crew she meant was herself, Lovella, Megan and Imogen. They were her crew. They were her people. She did not need anyone else. She wanted love, the romantic stuff like she had read in her favourite romance books, but she could not risk it, risk him being like- her obsessed one.

"I do not blame you for one minute. I can do more than that my Elfina." Lovella said warmly in a breeze. "I can bring wine, and I will bring plenty of it."

"Please, do." That would help. That would help indeed." That was what she needed right then. Company, positivity.

"Let us get shit faced."

She could say that again!

Elfina would need a whole bottle or five possibly of them, the way that she were then feeling inside, her nerves were in tatters after reading the letter aloud.

She reckoned that even a solo strip tease by the Chippendales wouldn't get a single smile out of her.

When all she wanted to now do were cry into her pillow and plan her next move. But why the hell should she?

After she hung up to her worried friend after signing off, she paced the spacious flat like a demented mad woman, searching in her mind for desperate answers to her desperate problem that never seemed to go away even though she desired it to.

A bazooka maybe? Or was that too extreme of a thing to use on?

Him. Why oh why!

She shivered.

Why couldn't he just die for crying out loud! She hoped that he burned! She would pay to see that, and she wasn't a violent soul.

She went carefully downstairs and went out the locked back door and let Sniggles do his poopy business in the small, private back yard behind her own place. For such a small dog he did not half do some humungous mountains of shite!

Not long after the door went with an agonising rap that made her heart pound with every knock that happened.

With a nervous twitch, she peered through the spy hole to see who it were there on the other side.

Oh, thank the lord! Her racing heart eased.

Her anxiety plummeted as she saw who it were there waiting impatiently. Her usually shy friend Megan lifted a bottle of glorious red wine and winked her way, as if she knew that she could see her through the hole, and they must have certainly heard her footsteps approaching.

She led them up and the four sat in the living room that she had not long redecorated to make the place her own. Gone were the granny wallpaper that had been there at first arrival and now it was a more elegant baby pink.

She liked pink. Who didn't?

Pink And black depending on what mood she were in.

Lovella had been straight on it once she had walked into the flat and had found some wine glasses from the kitchen to use and had then smacked the too many bottles of wine down that they had all brought with.

It did not matter either way. The perks of living in a city was that she could just run to the nearest off license not that far away if they ran dry. Not that she felt like going out after he had evaded her doorstep.

She might have to get her entrance hall and doorstep professionally cleaned!

Elfina herself was rather curvy and darn well proud of it, with long dark curly hair with a side line of frizz, and she had many tattoos, her most prominent was on her lower back that could be seen when she bent over in her usual casual vest top or blouse and loose boyfriend style jeans.

Well, she owned a tattoo shop after all and had to look the part! Couldn't exactly have a tattooist with no tattoos!

Most of them she had done herself- the ones that she could reach that were anyway. The back one would have been an impossibility!

She looked around at her friends who brought her so much joy in her sometimes-sad life.

Lovella. Dark skinned also curvy like Elfina were, ok -well plump, very sweet, very loud but funny, with dark afro hair that she envied more than anything in the world.

And she were- blunt.

Megan, usually shy, slim, shortish, black cleopatra like hair. Shy yes, but with a filthy sense of humour which Elfina adored so very much. If she needed cheering up or a wild night out at short notice and drinks being on tap, then Megan was her party girl.

Normally flicking through tinder and complaining about what was on offer on there, who was on there or about her bad dates that made her want to fucking scream. Of that there had been many.

That was not even before her poor friend got saddled with unwanted dick pics on there. Just why!

She wished that her friend could catch a break from being sent random un asked for cocks, bossy men, stinky ones, even cat fish ones. But for now, she had sworn off dating also. Elfina had not been on a date since he who should not be named by them had taken an unhealthy interest in her.

Nor she likely would. She was scared for herself but also scared for what he may do to her man if and when she got one. Was it fair to drag anyone into her mess?

No, no it wasn't.

Her other amazing friend Imogen, the blond also proud and out only lesbian of the group, slim and tall, who like the rest was also single and not quite sure if she wanted to yet mingle after her recent disappointing share of boo boos in the world of dating.

She was also seemingly having a bad time on the dating scene that she had become entangled in, going on to prove that even woman could be dickheads if they so wanted to be. But at least her bad dates didn't send random pictures of their lower lips to her.

In that her friend liking woman was somewhat blessed.

"So Elfina. Police or nah?"

Imogen asked this gazing at her as she gulped down her first glass of wine and then greedily held her glass out for yet more to be poured into it.

A light weight she was, so Elfina really wasn't sure about that being a good idea.

"No." She said firmly shaking her head from side to side at the police idea rather than the wine idea although both were a bad option in her opinion. "I don't want to taunt him. He would likely get off on it if I did so."

"He needs putting out. If I had five thousand free for a hitman for you and an alibi, his arse would be dead."

Lovella spat that uncharacteristically in all seriousness. Or if she had a gun, he would have likely met the end of it, and she wasn't even the violent type in any way that Elfina were aware of just like she herself weren't.

"Ha! I would give you the money if we got away with it!"

Cursed a becoming tipsy Elfina in agreement.

"Maybe he needs taunting." Continued on Imogen, about one of the worst men that she had the displeasure to ever met in her three-decade life. After all she had seen the way that the not even very handsome but smarmy guy kept popping up out from nowhere like a deranged rabbit out of a burning hat. Wishing that she could set fire to said hat and throw it into a mile long hole.

"Possibly." Elfina sighed sniffing the wine for a moment, scenting it, noticing it wasn't there usual brand that they tended to veer towards, more inferior than this one.

Was this what the cost of living had brought them too? Since she had brought the shop, she had had to be more careful with the coffers and so she could not go around randomly wasting money.

Elfina tapped her glass, "But no to the police. I have already tried that one out before as you know and he has way too many fingers in way too many pies, so it's no good there. Drink up girls, for right now I just want to get stone cold shit faced."

"Shit faced it is." Lovella smiled warmly with plump lips and with a cheeky clink to the other girls ones.

"What does the letter say?" Megan timidly asked her friend with a tilt of the head at her friend who were playing with the letter in her hands as though it were a hand grenade. Elfina quickly threw the crumpled-up letter her way, cos frankly she were done with it all, done with him, and her timid friend to her surprise caught it on first try.

Megan began to read it aloud, slurring as she went.

"I knew I would find you." Megan read out to the others. She frowned turning it over to surprisingly find merely a blank side there. "Is that it?" She turned it back over then handed it back.

Elfina nodded. "That's enough. Maybe I should move again?"

Megan crinkled her nose up on reading the letter, "God, he writes like a two-year-old. Heck even a two-year-old could write that better!"

Not that she had her own two-year-old. Or was sure if she wanted one.

"That is true. But moving. I need to get away." Elfina continued on in a fluster. She could feel her chest tightening which if she did not take control would lead to a full-blown panic attack... again.

"What, no!" Imogen said in absolute horror. "You have moved enough for that bloody, annoying man. I like it that you are closer to us now. To me." She smiled warmly.

Imogen lived the next road up. Lovella in the nearest town to Norwich and Megan the other side of the city near the airport. She herself lived in the city centre.

She were the only one of them to have no family left to speak of.

"Well then what to do I do?" Elfina asked the others as silence then hit the baby pink room. It bounced round and no one spoke.

What should she do?

CHAPTER TWO
IDEN

Iden had not liked the last run of the day at all much more than
the rest that he had had to deal with in the past eight hours of his soul-
collection work. Sometimes the soul that awaited him was ready for
completion when he got there right away, and yet at others the person
who awaited him was then hovering at the in between which were more
often than not.

A more callus vamp then him may have hanged around the near
body, waited until the final breath to make a move to the ready soul
so they did not have to deal with the humans last words whatever they
may be or their last fears.

So that they could take some of their blood from their neck or wrist
without question from the curious souls owner about why.

But he liked to see them off in this own particular way even if they
could not catch even a glimpse of him.

To let them know that they were not alone now when they neared
the very end of their life, in which there was no coming back from it.

The last journey of the day had been a small poorly terminally ill
child, a young lad, who had so desperately begged him to help them in
the hospital with their last shattered strength that they could muster
as they sensed him nearing them with a flap of invisible black feathery
wings.

Children seemed to sense way more about the unknown than the
adults humans did. Even animals were more aware then them and that
was saying something.

Iden had been so darn hungry and excited about having some more
blood to get him through the night in a more than peaceful state, but
even though his lips were now feeling cracked and dry, and his eyes
were now sunken into the sockets, then he would not inject his sharp
fangs into a recently gone child at all, even if they had consented him
to do so with a smile as they died.

The thought of doing it made him shudder; he would rather starve from lack of blood then do that monstrosity action.

He would not turn a child into a vamp either, for he were no monster although many over the years may have thought otherwise to that notion that knew him.

It were against the rules to do it so anyway.

To do so would be for selfish reasons and selfish reasons alone that he wanted no part to play in.

As their parents cries had rung out around them, the child had eventually gone off with him on his way to judgement with his help to, where he knew they would not long be starting life again in the upper realm, surrounded by the luxuries that they deserved to have for the rest of their time.

It was a shame that he would not be there to see it. Not be able to see them thrive and to grow.

Life had dealt a hard blow to the innocent child that they in no way had deserved.

There were indeed also no child vamps in his realm.

Nor would there ever be if so, he had his way. Yes, they could handle being a vamp he guessed that they could do, sucking blood straight from the source deliciously as they went and gaining many riches, niceties, a home of their own, their own family- like clan, as a reward for doing their job that they were required to do so for all of eternity.

But it was the job in itself that was no place for just a child.

Some of the horrors that he had seen in his oh so many years around as a gate keeper of souls had made even him wish that he had not been ever turned into a vamp by his own elder brother who at the time had not been so dark minded, a vamp who had to do this for there was no other, and he was lucky not to have been sucked into the darkness itself like the darkness vamps had done.

The bad guys who kept to the other end of the realm and thankfully kept to themselves most of the time.

The loners.

His brother Rhys was included.

He had not seen or heard from him since he left for there, nor did he want to now that he had heard what he had become on reaching there. He was now in charge of the darkness.

The darkness was him. He owned it with the dark magic he now wielded.

And he wanted his human mate, his human queen and had scoured the earth much like Iden himself had done for her but had apparently come up cold as well.

He was more like the humans version of vampires then Iden himself were.

Cold, bad, a blood sucking leech with no empathy to anyone or anything.

He himself was more like an angel crossed with a vamp, but he had been chosen and not quite born.

Vampires did not give birth nor could they.

They fucked, yes, gave birth and raise kids- no. It were impossible for a female vampire to.

Not long after arriving home the door to his large home flew open like a sudden gust of wind had, had at it.

What the! He wondered.

Sorcery of some kind for he knew there was some in existence? Or just a regular joe?

"Eh?" He scratched his head in confusion at the lack of visitor awaiting there and had an unsettled feeling deep in his stomach. Not that he wanted one right now – a visitor that were. His over workness was evident on him and his lack of blood was beginning to show up and cause signs and made him more easily irritated than usual.

No one to his surprise were there though!

What trickery was this he asked himself, as he then to his dis-amusement heard a scraping noise from somewhere behind him and spun round to face the music of who it truly were who had entered his home with invitation.

There a figure sat in a chair with one of his bottles of whisky in front of him and beside it were two short whisky glasses to match, one in each hand that were meant for only them.

It looked like he had been there for a while with how much were left in the bottle, but he had only just got there.

Did he not know how much that drink cost! Iden fumed.

Vamps did not get drunk, but they could get merrily tipsy, and this guy before him who he knew so well loved to drink more than anything else in the god forsaken realm!

Most people that knew him would hide the alcohol before he got around to theirs, or else he would most certainly wipe their alcohol store empty!

Or else a traipse to the large stores, full of all foods and drinks possible would be required to require some more.

Like a free Tesco. For vampires. Without a carpark as there were no cars there.

"Ashley." He grunted in displeasure.

He said this in slight annoyance to his now crimson eyed friend who he could see were guzzling his own finest whisky rather like it were merely only water.

"Iden."

His sort of friend said in return with a sharp fanged grin that showed that he had not long fed.

The jammy bugger. Iden himself needed some bad but it would have to wait.

"What have I told you about just waltzing into my home and making yourself comfy there?" Iden scolded him. "This is becoming a habit, my very annoying dear friend."

He gestured around his large spectacular home.

The one that was supposed to be all his and his alone. He wanted that.

He needed it. He had earned the right to have his own space in this realm! Somewhere just for him. To lay low. To enjoy the never-ending silence that he so often enjoyed.

But never got.

But even though he liked the solitude, the quiet to think sometimes, process all the going ons, and the clan all knew it, he was frequently dropped into by thankless visitors.

With thankless questions.

Like didn't they all have anywhere else that they could be rather then darkening his huge door instead of elsewhere?

His house breaker friend Ashley or Ash also had a rather nice home to call his own though not as splendid as his were of course what with being the clan Fortheart leader.

They all did.

His one you could walk into or even fly into from entry up top. Surrounded by beautiful pillars and stunning statues that he had collected over the years.

Ok, nicked...

Poor wasn't a thing there in the vampire realm like the human world and money was no object because they didn't actually require it there.

What was the interest in his home instead of his he thought as he eyed his friends pausing from drinking his whisky and looking around his home?

Ashley had annoyingly turned up many, many times out of the blue un- invited without no reason to name of but mere excuses to be there to see him.

Ashley was an interesting dark-skinned male. Interesting were putting it mildly in most people's opinions. But he was a good bloke, or vamp or whatever you liked to call him.

Similar build to him but with cat like eyes that bore into you as if he were actually feline, he were also so quick to move like a cat too which were how he had got onto the chair in that short amount of time and drunk down the booze that was not even his, in one greedy gulp.

If Iden were gay which he wasn't, he really wasn't, then this fine dark-skinned prince like devil there would tempt him in every way possible because he was so annoyingly perfect to look at.

It was only his drinking habit that needed working on.

But he wasn't interested in doing that.

Ashley poured Iden a drink as though it were he that lived there in the old mansion instead of him. Iden`s blood was now boiling much like a kettle reaching its relentless boiling point that would soon peak.

"Thank you I guess." Ash just smiled eagerly at his friend.

Iden himself cautiously took the glass from his friends awaiting fingers whilst dreaming about stabbing his cheeky friend with it cold heartedly instead. Twisting the glass into his dead heart.

It were a shame he thought that the only way to kill a vamp was to actually set them on fire until they turned to mere ash or to fully decapitate them so that their head left their body.

Never to return to it.

Stabbing him would just merely piss him off!

Maybe.

He knew that Ashley had a high tolerance to others antics and would likely fight back in his own, silly way and take it as a joke if it happened. They had been friends for eons upon eons so things between them both were easily forgiven.

Even attempted murder he guessed.

Ashley frowned at his slick back haired, friend in what seemed to be friendly concern.

"You know... You look like you could do with some blood my friend. Things been, ok? You have had plenty of souls to collect from what I gathered today, seeing you fly off here, fly off there so I don't understand why you are this way?" He pointed at Iden who was shaking slightly from blood shortage.

Most wouldn't notice the symptoms that were beginning to show themselves except those who knew him really well that he was obviously becoming blood deprived.

Iden shrugged, "It was mainly just the elderly and kids today that I collected, and time were short. I was not taking blood from those kind of mortals. It would not be right for me to. My heart is dead but still as of yet, I am not heartless."

"I appreciate the predicament mate, but you need it. We need it. They would understand. They have to. It is us and all that we are." Ashley said, trying to get his clan leader to see sense.

"No. It is not the way." On that Iden remained firm. His mind would not be changed.

"But I..."

"But you yourself would?" Iden snapped out. "That's your decision right there Ash. Whatever helps you to sleep soundly at night. Or day...I would rather sleep in my crypt at night knowing that I have done the right thing by me, by others, then to take blood from those that don't deserve me to take it from them. Blood from innocent children? The thought of it sickens me and I have never feasted on a minor. The elderly? They fought in the war for the humans freedom. It is not right, and it never will be right to gorge on their crimson goodness."

Ash nodded.

He knew his friend were right, but Ashley's love of blood outweighed his morals.

"All those souls that piled up in the second world war that we struggled to collect... the survivors to that war do not deserve that. To be used as our blood bags. No. Not I."

"Fair enough then. Changing the subject here before you self-combust, and we throw punches again like before...I have some news that I wanted to share with you. It is not pleasant, but it is still news," Ashley said, his eyes zoning in on his friends just like he could read his own mind and pluck out his every thought and decipher it.

Maybe he could...more stranger things had happened in their hidden world. More stranger things were yet to come.

But they did not know it...

"Go on..."

Iden urged him, wanting to know what brought him to his home that very day. Again, for he had already popped in earlier that day when they both had a break between their souls. "Out with it....NOW."

Ashley did not answer though straight away and instead got up in a speedy vamp flash like blur and walked over to a large bay window where he then stood silently and watched outside like it were a prize.

Iden had had enough after a few moments and gripped his hands together in his impatience.

"You know impatience is..."

"Your middle name, yeah, I know. Also, it`s blah blah blah." Ashley taunted him.

"Your skating on very thin ice here Ash."

"Well, my friend that is the best ice to skate on I do believe." Ash said with a firm smirk.

"True."

They both liked a challenge although falling through the ice and becoming stuck under water would not kill them in any way, it instead would be a living horror for them to be alive under the water, being thirsty and wishing for death that would never come with no way to ever get out of there.

No way to get their much-desired blood that gave them their boost of power.

Vampires could not die from lack of blood, no, but they could get very sick without it after a period of time and would become almost – frozen in time. Sometimes they could also go the other way and go feral if that happened, and in a few cases, feral vamps had sadly had to have been put down by others in their clan because they had had to of.

There had been no other option but to dispose of them for the goodness of all others around them. Blood lust was a terrible thing.

If they became a risk in the human world, then that could be the end of them.

Ashley after his endless silence which were unlike him- then sprung it on him. Knowing that this piece of info would temporarily turn Iden`s world upside down because it involved something that he wanted- but had not found yet.

A treasure that they all wanted.

"Geoffrey has found his human mate." Ashley said quietly.

"What!"

Iden hissed out in outrage and then speedily himself zoomed over to Ashley's ready form and then put a firm hand onto his bulky shoulder where he kept it there firmly, with a gentle grip of the claws that came out.

"How?" Also, in a mad beckoning hiss. "And who? Who is she that has captivated him in this way?" Iden did not mean to snap this time at his second, he really did not, but his apparent anger was coming out now and it would not stop as the whole searing jealousy that he felt coarse through him, as it unsettled him even more so.

As it did each time that a younger vamp, heck even an older vamp then him found their human mate and not he or even someone that he cared deeply for such as those who had fought battles with him over the years.

They all remained- simply loveless though. If he had his way all in the realm would find their other half – and soon.

Why couldn't it be him! Blood Geoffrey! Why him?

He threw his whisky glass madly across the room and his mild-mannered friend then winced as it shattered hard like his leaders dead heart had just gone and done.

Would there ever be anyone to repair it? They both felt the same way though. They both shared the same opinion. They did not need to say otherwise.

Why had the meek boring Geoffrey met the other part of him? Why not someone that actually deserved it?

Who had earnt it.

These two there had been patiently waiting for hundreds if not thousands of years for their human mate to be found by them.

Loved by them, cherished in every way that were truly possible.

What would they look like?

Iden was not fussy about who she were that much as long as they were his and his alone which they would be, he would ensure that, but he was usually into curvy woman, and he also preferred dark haired to those fair.

Skin colour was of no importance to him either. His dark-skinned friend Ashley was equal to him.

Every day that they both spent their days soul collecting and both silently wished that this would be it for them to find her.

The day that their mate saw them.

Saw them for who they really were.

All of them. Forever. Their human one.

They would then remain not invisible to a human no longer than that.

Geoffrey was barely fifty years past bitten and were frankly in most of the clans view dull as dish water, and in Iden`s opinion that were being polite and then some added to it.

No one had to his knowledge found their mate in a long while.

"I feel sorry for his mate. What a drip!"

Ashley sniggered this into his own near empty whisky glass with lowered eyes, while Iden ignored the glass strewn floor around them or also the fact that his fingers were now profusely bleeding a weird purple shade of blood and went on to make another drink for himself.

He needed it.

But truthfully, he needed blood way more. What he wouldn't do for some right about then. Iden`s eyes bulged at the thought of it making its way into his mouth.

Iden did not say anything else until he were clutching another drink tight in his grasp but the silence between them was in no way awkward.

But necessary.

The two had of them been through too many things together over the years for things to ever be that awkward. More of an irritation shall we say.

Iden thought about Ashley's words and said, "On that I agree. But why not us dear Ashley? What have we done to deserve the wait for our beloved mate, our one, for so long? Are they even out there for us to find?"

"That I don't know. That I don't know." Ashley shrugged sighing miserably as the stance changed in the room to one of sheer gloom with no hope in between.

It should be their reward for the years of hard work, dark work that they had to do every day, day in day out with only evenings and the night to recover from it in anyway.

A mate. Forever.

Someone to share their eternal life with.

But there it had fell flat.

They did not dare take a chosen mate, because sods law- she, his fated one would then turn up. And if he had to make a choice there was only one that he could possibly ever make.

Iden was the one now in charge of a quarter of the realm, there were four main clans, well five including the nameless part, although they let the darkness part do their own thing with their own clan and it had been apart from the rest of the realm for many years since the peace fell apart.

Evaporated into thin air.

He did not want to be consumed by that over whelming blackness that lingered on in there. The powers that verged into witchcraft. It was not for their world.

But now it were. He wanted no part of that.

Ashley was his side in line, his aide if you liked and so he brought him important news when there was any to be brought.

Like that specific piece of unsuspected gossip that made him want to hunt Geoffrey down right then and to punch him square in the nose.

Geoffrey, would he gathered presumably want to go on to leave the realm he so guessed as his mate could not stay there with him by each other's side.

She would not even be able to see the realm without being a proper vamp or a regular blood drinker anyway, and she would not be safe to do so if she could.

She would be a walking meal for those who could not control their blood lust. They could not risk that.

"Come on mate." Ashley added. "It's not like we are going to miss much if he leaves here! He`s boring as shit. The place will liven up if he goes."

"When he goes."

Ok when he goes. But he is dull as dish water. Whoever created him needs shooting. He does as well."

"True. That is true!" Iden said with a slight chuckle.

It were his own brother who had turned the boring ass vamp that was about to sail off into the sunset with a mate of their own.

His own sire at that.

Unlike him he had only turned those who he felt deserved a second chance, no they needed it. Rhys turned those that would make the vamp realm a darker more vicious place to live.

The stuff of legends.

Except for Geoffrey that were. It would always remain a mystery why he had even been turned into what he were now. He did not have a single ounce of badness from what Iden had seen or heard of him.

As the friends bonded, moaned together and groaned, the door to his dismay went yet again with a start.

"Hope they don't want any of your whisky!" Ashley laughed naughtily. Iden spun around from looking at the knocked door to the bottle which now lay empty and discarded.

"Jesus Ash." He muttered under his breath.

Next time he got some he would have to lock it away out of reach of wandering clawed hands.

Before he could answer it, the door swung open. In walked a dark-haired small build female, that was much a sister to him and Geoffrey and Barren behind her. She was the only one that could barge into his house openly through the front door without him being tempted to break their teeth in.

To shatter their jaw.

Ruby.

He had sired her five years ago now and had not regretted it even for a single moment or a single breath.

"Hi Iden." She grinned it warmly as she came in donning a messy bun and a flowery patterned summer dress with the other two standing behind her like her own puppies as they watched her in what could only be described as sheer awe. Both the other two were not as brave as to barge in to the head of their clans vampires lair without an invite.

Ruby however much like Ashley did not give much of a shit.

He did not like to think as himself with any fancy titles. Iden thought that they should all be one big, happy family and try to solve things together and amicably if they could.

No such luck there.

FIVE YEARS AGO.

Once Ruby had had time to settle into the whole vampire realm and her shockingly spectacular white wings had grown out from behind her petite back and she had gotten used to using them, then they had gone on the hunt together for vengeance.

The hunt for the four men.

The ones who had wrecked her life, lost her, caused her life to cease, and now she would wreck theirs just as they had done so hers.

Forever. Whereas she had died whole, she knew that those four men would be someday soon found in mere broken pieces. Either whole or apart. She had not figured that out yet.

"Please come with me. I don't want to face them alone." Ruby had looked up at Iden, her hero, not that she would tell him, with her usual long - lashed puppy dog eyes that he knew were all for show for his benefit.

She had developed pure strength since on becoming a vamp that she had so desperately needed to, and he knew there were now little that scared her.

Except this. Seeing those disgusting men again.

"You sure?" He eyed her cautiously.

"Positive." She had nodded and then bit noisily into her red juicy apple.

Red like the blood of the damned. The blood that they both know would spill that very night. He would enjoy every mouthful of it.

"Ruby, I wouldn't miss it for the world."

His eyes had lit up brightly to crimson red, which only happened after feeds or during pure anger usually, and his mouth had grinned wickedly at the thought of what was to come that evening.

Meal time. A four-course meal at that.

He did not cherish the blood of the wicked normally for his consumption but for her, for his needs also, he would turn a blind eye to where it had really come from.

Ashley or Barren would not have given a shit and would have likely also joined the party if they had been invited to it, which they hadn`t of been.

The bad men ripping up party.

But this was Rubys revenge to give. One that she had asked him and only him, to be part of. Iden, her sire, was the only one that knew the exact details that had happened on her change from human to vampire night.

It was not his place to tell. Not his place to act.

But hers.

She had paced around his home nervously with a nibble of her lips. She lived not far from his he wouldn't have it any other way, she was much like the bratty little sister that he never had. His had been more to do.

Rest her young innocent soul.

Plus, she didn't fancy him like most the other female vampires did that he knew of, and he wasn't being big – headed there.

Iden could have vamp pussy whenever he wanted to.

But It bored him to be honest after so many years of trying this and that and going round again and ending up back at before.

On top, under and everything in between.

He liked the chase instead of it being to him handed cheekily on a platter. Where could he find a girl like that?

Would his mate be a chaser or a runner?

"They won't be able to see me, will they?" Ruby had asked him with a brief moment of fear on her brave, pale face. Her moment of weakness now arising from out of the blue. Her thoughts of revenge slipping and turning into panicked thoughts.

Iden smiled in sympathy.

"No. As I explained that is not how it works. The only way that they could see you is if they became a vamps mate or a vamp themselves. If that were the case and I saw them anywhere near here, me or you, this bloody realm, then I would bludgeon them to death myself with my trusty pick axe." He pointed to it in the corner on display.

His most favourite of tools. He even preferred it to his swords.

"Thanks, Iden. Can I borrow your axe?" She winked with a finish.

"No." He growled. Anything but that.

"Aww. No fair!" She jested.

"I would do anything for you. Except that. That axe is my baby." Because he would. Because it were.

She gazed up at him with a small, sweet smile in return at their platonic friendship that she treasured also dearly. Having only being blessed with a sister, he was indeed like a big brother.

Protective, fierce, loyal.

"You too." And she meant it. With every fibre of her eternal soul.

At first after her change into something else besides mortal, she had been slightly worried that his interest in her, his closeness to her, his reason for changing her was due to him having a possibly romantic interest in her.

That was until she realised that he were waiting patiently for his human mate.

And it was not she.

Apart from one-night fangs, friends with blood benefits and also mad and crazy wing flings- he was waiting for his only one to be by his side for all of eternity and the back of beyond.

She hadn't even had to divulge to him, to tell him about her own particular tastes, he had guessed from the very off of her rainbow frilled secret.

Her identity.

The fact that she only liked the ladies.

Blonde ones.

They set off for their night of expectant, blood filled fun.

It had not been long of searching, waiting, watching, before they had found the unsuspecting, disgusting men with their disgusting vile scent, and the bonus was, the four were all huddled together and in a relatively quiet place.

The two blood sucking vampires had stood watching them obviously undetected for a long while she plucked up the courage to begin her blood quest.

Her feast, their demise.

He said what was on his mind before they struck the scum down. He could feel her tense up, her walls going back up. To protect her mind from unravelling, being swept away after what had happened that day.

"Now then, what are we going here with Ruby? Death or just taking these monsters to near death? Or just a bit of limb ripping here and there? Could shove a leg up their own arses?"

Iden joked in all seriousness.

She laughed quickly at that thought cos it was bloody funny, but the memory of her assault five years ago, and the worry that they had maybe done it to others still remained so close to the surface, and she faltered for a brief moment.

She froze.

She looked at him, her painted lashes firmly down.

Then she looked up at her sire with an evil grin. "Why, death of course my sire."

That was his girl.

They had taken her virginity, her choice, they had trod on her own sure sexuality as though it were merely nothing to them or any other. She had never been interested in men in that way, never would do, never had wanted that path to follow, this way.

Or that.

He did not blame her in any way for the death and pain that she wanted to bring to these mere scum huddled in a group trading weed, booze and fags.

He had feared that if she had not taken her own form of revenge that night then he would have dealt his own form of punishment out to them eventually.

But she was. It were time.

"Let's get those cock suckers."

"Lets."

They laughed with every second of the men's agonising fear filled screams that wailed unanswered throughout the lonely cool night, and they felt- they felt nothing inside.

Only pure joy. Did that make them bad? No, it made them vengeful...

Nothing deep inside, it was if their insides were cold.

Because to them what they were doing was so, so right in every way. Not wrong at all like it actually truly were.

No guilt, no remorse, no second thoughts about the whole entire thing. In fact, she wished that she had taken the raging bull by the horns and done it all sooner.

It felt way more violent to her she had said later because the sickening, murdering rapists could not see the two attack them from out of the blue, who both simply just chuckled as they sucked their scummy blood dry, blood were dripping everywhere freely, dripping around in their increasing ecstasy and after they had gotten their fill, watched as they shit themselves to death in fear- they left them there on the floor in a cold-hearted heap clumped together.

Dead as a dodo.

Left for the police to have the dis pleasure of finding.

And there had been nothing that the men could have done about it. Nothing could have saved them from their planned-out fate.

NOTHING. Because they simply -deserved it. Every rip, every tear every cry.

They had, had no chance against the two of them. The two would not be taking their souls in either to be judged for what came after next, and these vamps could face repercussions for that, repercussions for the sheer brutal murder that they had inflicted on the men.

For murder was a crime in their realm even if dealt by a clan leader or by their associates. Not soul collecting without good reason was also a serious crime. But It would be one that they faced - together.

And together they so did.

Now

Iden let the three guests in begrudgingly and slammed the door to with a large, booted foot. He went over to his large favourite, decision making chair, and sat down onto the cushioned seat and wiggled his pert bum.

He glowered at them all with a hard arsed look, until one of the three actually said their reason for them being there in his space.

One soon spoke. They could feel his fury mounting like a fiery volcano, but they did not know why, how or what had caused this.

It was the female of the group who had the balls to speak first.

"Iden, me and Barren have a request for you. We would like to be able to leave the realm now that our work here is done for the day." Ruby said. "I think that we have earned some free time away to relax and unwind someplace else."

"Go on. Why are you asking for permission Ruby? You aren't children!" Iden sighed and the room stilled and waited.

Knowing that it would be something that they wanted that he did not care for or that he would want to hear.

It always were.

They knew how to push him, to push his buttons until he cracked up and lost his cool.

Sometimes he thought that they irritated him on purpose, for the kicks of it.

Or else they would not take no for an answer.

Ashley laughed out loud behind him where he stood stone faced with a grim expression and Iden glanced at him in complete and utter displeasure.

He had come in, stolen his booze and was now laughing at his expense! The nerve of it!

In clan leader mode instead of as a simple friend now he glowered. They were both, the leader and his second, now more than used to Ruby and Barren's crazy ass requests to leave the realm for a time.

A new theme park opening that they had noticed when visiting the human world?

They wanted in! A theatre outing?

Yeah, that interested them too! Why couldn't they do the things that they had there?

In his view they should stay all away from the mortal bearing humans, their world, unless one was their mate, or else if they were doing their soul job and so had to be.

Ruby and Barren wanted to be free to go there as often as they wanted to without any requirements attached.

To even visit their family.

She, her beloved still breathing sister.

Iden had said that that was not the way to do things. That they mustn't. If family and friends sensed them, it could scare them, they could unintentionally unveil their secret to the world which could cause absolute uproar. The humans did not know that vamps truly existed, and they were still hidden by their invisibility from them.

It was too dodgy for his liking. Their family, friends, co-workers, neighbours Barr Ruby, thought they were all - dead. It was time that they acted like it. He had outlived all his companions, parents, his sister, all except his brother.

Even this request from her surprised him.

"I...I..."

"We would like to go see the super Mario movie tonight." Chirped in Barren bravely to the saga as Ruby stumbled for the right words to say to her scowling sire. He added- "And the coronation of the king the weekend after if you please. I would like to see his majesty get crowned."

Why? Iden himself was more of a Diana fan.

There was a long pause while Iden picked his jaw up off the floor.

He did not speak. Not say a word. It was Geoffrey who they had all forgotten was there with them already who broke the stunned silence in the leaders home.

"What planet are you two on?"

Ashley side eyed the other two. He seemed to have found another bottle of whisky from somewhere much to Iden's displeasure, but he were too busy glaring at the others to mention it.

He noted it for later though. Maybe he could lace a bottle with arsenic? Watch his friend with eagle eyes choke and gasp, fall down, but then eventually resurface to drink all his booze again.

Ashley scoffed, "For once I actually agree with something that you said Geoffrey. I never thought I would see the day."

"No. Absolutely not," That was Iden that said that.

The boss.

"Watch it on the telly like everyone else here who wants to. And wait for Mario to be released on DVD. You have a built-in cinema at the back of your home."

"But I..." Ruby argued. She had been here before. She likely would again.

They all had. She was what they classed as a baby vamp, she was still finding her feet between being a vamp and being human. "There's no people there."

"So? You are better off without them. Trust me. People suck."

"But that's the fun of days out. Being around people."

"They can't see you, Ruby."

She lowered her head. "Oh, I know!" Iden did feel remorse then at the pained expression on her beautiful face.

"So, what joy do you get in it?" He clicked his fingers. He himself would rather watch films in peace then surrounded by people chewing on popcorn noisily, the over bearing loudness of the film and kids that yelled and messed about during an important scene.

Yeah no. He was alright there thanks.

"I didn't asked to be turned by you Iden!" She shouted.

Wow he thought, the ungrateful little madam!

Iden put a firm hand on a trousered hip. Why oh why, was he the leader of this moronic clan he was beginning to wonder as the blood desire hit, and her ungratefulness increased it. How could he have let her die! She didn't deserve that as a death. No one did!

He eyed her, "If I was to say no, would you still go ahead and go to the human realm anyway without my say so involved?"

"No..." She didn't sound too sure of it.

Ruby said this at the same time as Barren muttered defiantly

"Maybe we would..."

He was asking for trouble right there. He could have least lied and denied that they would even attempt to go when they had been declined.

"Perhaps some time in the jail might do you both the world of good?" Iden had done it to his own before. Hauled them off for time out in the deep, dark dungeons.

He would do it again. His clan had a few thousand at least and they did not all toe the line.

What would it take to make them see that their idea of just a simple bit of humorous fun at the movies, a fun night out, could bring the destruction of them all?

Their doom.

They were invisible vampires with wings for fucks sake!

They might have the upper hand what with being invisible to most of the humans in the blue, glorious green world, but they knew the humans that if they knew about them could stop them doing their job in the way that it needed to be done.

If the souls weren't collected by them, then there would be hell to pay. Life as they all knew it would be over.

The world needed balance. The balance was them.

It was everything about them.

It was all who they were. All they could ever be. They needed the job, needed the blood to get by and to live.

Needed the consistency.

"You wouldn't," Ruby gasped, paling at the thought of some jail time for her and her posh friend. She had seen others suffer the same fate, but she had not in her opinion done anything bad enough to warrant time behind bars there.

Would he though?

She didn't think that he would, but he was pretty darn angry right then at her and at Barren. Her especially. She knew for certain the raging envy he felt at Geoffrey. She had seen it before.

She had caught him at a bad moment it had seemed as she backed away. Maybe they should have left it alone for a time?

"Oh, that got your attention then young Ruby." Iden swiftly got up and started pacing the room like an angry Jackal gunning for a fight. A thing that they all knew him doing, meant they had gravely overstepped the mark there, and that he was now less than one step away from making the whisky glass shattering incident that Ash had witnessed back then look like child's play and then him blowing an expected gasket.

"Maybe leave our clan and join the darkness one if you like breaking the rules here where I am the one in charge. This clan, us, tries to keep to the rules if we can do so. It is what is expected of us. It is my rules. My way. Or the highway."

She gasped in answer at pent up frustration. Her face monster like.

"Bloody man! I would never join them! I would rather die than join them!"

She would. She wasn't lying there. She were a good girl, they knew that – well most of the time....

He gave her a warped look. "Your already dead Ruby." And three, two, one....

"Wow. You actually went there, didn't you?" She could not believe that he had uttered that one. He knew that that would hurt her. Pull at what was left of her insides.

Oh dear.

Iden rolled his eyes, "Yes, yes, I did. And now if you are done having your poxy ass tantrum, I think we are all done here somewhat. I have had a rather shit day and it is now still getting shitter or so it seems to be what with drama at my door."

"Well, I'm not going anywhere, you stubborn arse jerk!" Ruby fumed. "And that's your job. As sire, as leader. Your bloody job!"

The two rarely argued so this was one of the rare occasions that they did so to speak of.

Three of them in the room stood glowering at each other with no let up to it happening anytime soon. Maybe even ever. While one other tried to catch the clan leaders eye and the other male drunk and drunk till the cows came home regardless, and then drunk some more just to be on the safe side of that.

Ash could keep a pub in business just by himself.

That was if they had pubs in the realm. Or money. Who needed cash when they were instructed to collect souls by a higher being then them?

They didn't sadly for him have pubs there.

So instead, he went round his friends' homes and drunk all their alcohol or nicked some from the earth stores on his essential visits there. Maybe he could build his own pub?

Iden didn't know why he hadn't personally. Not many wanted to work, they had enough on.

He sat back in the chair with a slouch.

"Anyway, if you are all finished squabbling. About me?" Geoffrey piped in, not quite reading the room right then.

Or not caring either way.

"Shut up Geoffrey." The others snaped in unison at him. He flinched.

"But my Susan. I need to be with my dear Susan. She needs me. She will be lost without me." He said this as almost a strangled cry. He whined.

They all strongly doubted that last one. They pitied poor Susan already. She had possibly gone into hiding to avoid him and his simpering.

"Who the fucks Susan?" Snapped Iden. Oh, he knew. He knew all right!

He pounced out of his seat like a lion ready to strike a meal, and headed straight for the startled Geoffrey who cowered and lowered his head in total submission. Iden's face changed from handsomely something else to something more like a humans version of a demon.

Geoffrey flustered, "My mate. She is my mate. I have met my human mate, sir at long last. I also have a piece offering for you Iden, before I go." He smiled weakly.

"At long last! At long last! You have been here the same amount of time that Barren had not changed his underwear! And go? Who said you could go anywhere? Aren't you on soul shift still? Are you slacking while the others take the fall for it?" Iden was nearly nose to nose with the bumbling idiot, but he did not care.

He could taste his stale breath in the chilly air.

"No, no sir." Geoffrey shook his head. "But she can't come here. So, I will have to go there."

It was the only way.

"Tough." Spat out Iden. He did not care. Not his circus, maybe his monkey though.

Geoffrey looked like one. Hairy.

Maybe Iden wasn't being fair. He knew somewhere in his cold, still heart that he wasn't being it. But the envy was taking over him like it lived inside him, and it would just get worse, and worse until he found – her.

His love.

He was pining for something that he did not yet know of. But that he wanted to. So very much. It might make him sad, not much of a vamp. He did not care, he wanted her.

"Iden. Let him be. He has what we want but that is no reason to not to give him his own chance of happiness." Barren said.

"Fuck off Barren." Ashley said, actually stopping drinking to cuss at him with a dangerous glint in his eye. His loyalty with Iden where it would always lay.

The black hottie and the dark haired posh one stood face to face, eye to eye.

Not one of them giving in. Not one likely would.

The room was full to the brim of over bearing male tension.

"Make me." A shuddering hiss. Fangs shot out with a clash.

"You bet I would!" A snapped retort.

"How did she take you being a vamp?" Iden's face softened as he interrupted the fighting. It were a question that they had all wondered. They all stopped and looked at the hairy vamp with questions in their eyes.

Geoffrey paled. The answer was one that he was yet to like.

"I... I haven't told her yet. I didn't know what to say. But she saw the wings. My wings. She knows that we are connected somehow, but not quite why or how. I wanted to tell you, to ask you first to go and for you to listen. I also wanted to give you this."

Geoffrey reached into his own pocket of his trousers and took out a small vial of blood from it. He handed it straight to Iden who he knew needed it, they all did, who snatched it out of his hand impatiently with flashing eyes.

Iden drunk the red delicious nectar down greedily with a gulp.

He did not care that the others looked on. He drunk the small, but good enough for him vial and he thanked the lord for bringing him Geoffrey.

He now felt so much better after that.

The rage left him and he had a clear mind that could think properly again. Yes, yes of course he were jealous of the buffoon who were now - his surprising saviour.

He handed a hand out to a stunned Geoffrey. The clan leaders face then returned to his usual one.

Handsome again. Not as scary looking. Still mean though.

Geoffrey took it with no hesitation and shook it firmly.

"Congratulations Geoffrey. We will still see you at the monthly clan meetings still I take it?" Iden said frankly.

"Yes, yes of course Iden." The beaming man gave him a polite nod.

"Well good luck. If she is meant for you, then she will accept you being a vamp. For it is what you are. Be you and she will see you. Hide yourself and she won't."

"I hope so."

"And thank you." Iden said.

For if wasn't a snickers when he was hungry that he had needed but some blood. They all did. But Iden even though he could go for a lot longer than others without it often pushed himself to go longer and longer until he snapped.

Did he like that crippling edge? Maybe.

Some of them stored spare blood in their homes, in large fridges, he often did or got it from fresh while out if the moment struck him.

He often bit the body of the soul he collected or else he hunted like a predator for someone worthy of a good biting.

The drunk older teens were the best bet for a good old gnaw. Drunk as to not realise what was going on when they were bit out of the blue and drunk enough so that no one believed them.

Plus, the buzz from the alcohol in their system was nice.

Drugs through his system was a firm no- no. He would not touch drug addled blood with a barge pole. Nor would he take any himself.

Iden tapped the soon departed one hard on the shoulder with a now clawed finger. Knowing that as a vamp they had speedy healing, and it would not matter how hard he smacked that quaking shoulder for he would bounce back.

"I know so. Now then. You three go to your homes, gather the locals or who else wants to come and let's get a farewell party started at the field! By the way I am out of alcohol through no fault of my own, and I do not have the time to restock today all thanks to a certain someone who shall remain nameless."

They all turned to Ashley who burped unashamedly and hid his blushing chiselled face with a hand.

His face then went blank, he stilled, and they all got back to their business as a few mere minutes later Ashley leapt off on out on soul collecting business.

While they planned a fair well. But in there lay hope that they all might meet their fated ones themselves someday.

Before it were too late...

CHAPTER THREE

E LFINA
The next day Elfina with a slightly sore head, opened her shop up. Her first tattoo of the day was actually for Imogen who had stayed the night due to this specific appointment but had then got up early to go for a run, and for what she guessed was for - her usual morning cake.

Imogen ate far more then Elfina did but was still a few sizes slimmer! Life wasn't fair. Elfina guessed that she had the metabolism of a slug compared to her lean friend!

On time as usual, Imogen was already leaning against the painted shop wall outside the shop with a hint of crumbs on her lips.

"You missed a bit." Elfina grinned and nodded towards her friend's pouted mouth.

"Oh, darn it!" Imogen wiped her mouth with a manicured hand and laughed.

"Why didn't you just knock me up?"

"Kinky."

"No, I didn't mean that... Doesn't matter. Please do come in." Elfina gestured inside to her friend and got into shop owner mode. "Now sit."

"You sober enough to do this?" Imogen teased her. The night before had ended up lairy. At least that was one thing they could thank that dickhead for – bringing four friends even closer together.

"Yes." Elfina rolled her eyes.

"That is a relief. Now the tat that I have picked...." There was a pause.

"Yes?" Elfina hesitated with a curious gaze. She really wanted Imogen to be sure of her decision. Yes, of course she needed the customers, the money, the hope that they came back and recommended her to friends, as times had been tough for all since 2020 and the covid epidemic that ran though the world. But without laser treatment they were talking of a permanent thing to mark themselves with really.

She did not want her chum to live to regret it.

"Do you think it's a bit much?" Imogen asked in all seriousness.

Elfina thought about the big, bright, rainbow tat that Imogen wanted on her mid-thigh. It would be very bright; it would be very big.

She thought for a moment as simply a best friend rather than a mere shop owner doing business. She thought it were pretty cool an idea herself, but would Imogen live to regret it if she rushed into it?

Was it something that suited her, meant something to her?

It would, and it did.

"No. It's perfect." A single tear shed from the tattooist's eye that rolled down her cheek. Her emotions were always all over the place after drinking and that day were no different to usual. And last night after the jerk had gone to her flat, invaded her safety, her home, the fact he had found her again frankly she had needed it.

Imogen raised a blonde groomed brow, "Really? You don't think it's a bit... bit too gay?"

Well, that was completely unexpected.

Elfina pulled back her head and laughed wickedly for a moment. Imogen just gawped at her for a moment as her friend got the giggles.

She tried to compose herself, "Sorry, I wasn't laughing at you Imogen. No, it is not too gay! It is just you. You to a tee. I don't know if I ever told you as she is hard to talk about, but my sister is... or was also a lesbian. She would have fucking loved the idea of your tat although she wasn't as strictly as confident in her sexuality as you are, likely due to our arse hole parents and their old-fashioned ways."

"Was?" Imogen tilted her head in interest. "What happened to her, love?"

Elfina had met Imogen through Megan and Lovella not long after her sisters suspected passing five years ago, so she likely did not even know that she had a sister. Or still did anyway, for she did not know what had actually happened to her, there was no body to bury, no place to say her last tearful goodbyes and to mourn her forever more.

But she strongly suspected with all of the evidence that the police had, and the lack of contact from her sister that she had sadly passed on.

Her sister never would have left her willingly or for long periods of time that was for sure because of how close they were. Barely a day went past that she was not on the phone to her before she vanished that sad day.

Elfina lowered her gaze, "It's not a very nice story mate to be honest, I don't want to bring you down with it. You are here for something new. Sadly, her story is something old and depressing." That were the truth. With knobs on.

"You aren't. You won't," Imogen was becoming curious now and put her chin in her hands. She had always known that Elfina had a troubled life with her family, she knew that her parents had been complete and utter bigoted dickheads, but she had never opened up to her about her sister.

Like there were something that had happened to her sibling that was much too upsetting to say to anyone out loud...

Her friend was struggling with where to begin her tale as she kept opening and shutting her mouth like a guppy goldfish. If to begin. How to even.

"It's bad, Gem."

"Open up to me Elfina. Please."

Elfina began the story slowly but surely, "My lovely sister, she is missing but presumed dead and the police have recently closed the case. Her blood and DNA was sadly found in an alley way with torn clothing and with the DNA of disgusting, multiple men on it. It looked to be like she had been assaulted and then presumably... killed." She gulped down her anguish and trembled down her fear.

Her over whelming urgent need to know what had happened to her sister. Nobody wanted to lose a sibling, of course not, no one did but it would be much better knowing the truth about what had happened that faithful night then not knowing at all. She needed answers.

But it looked like none were coming to her.

It was always so hard to talk about to anyone, to voice aloud, because it hurt so bloody much as it should do to say that her sweet sister had gone.

"Strangely the men that were suspected of harming her were all later found murdered by what looked like a ferocious animal. It had torn them apart. Their DNA was only linked to her attack after it was compared later on after their brutal death. One that I am glad happened to them it was the least they deserved after what they did to my sister."

"I am so sorry I did not know of this." Imogen put a hand on her friend`s own one and squeezed it gently. "At least they went out In the most painful way possible that they all truly deserved to." Her eyes glistened with tears badly.

Elfina liked the sound of that also, "That my friend is true. Now then let's get this awesome tat done, I am done talking about those evil fuckers." Her friend nodded.

Continuing, "It is making me want another tat it really is seeing your design."

Imogen shuffled in the seat trying to get comfy, "You should. Get a really loud and proud gay one, just for your sweet sister. And fuck your parents."

Sharp and to the point. But true.

"They are gone too. They died not knowing what happened to her."

Imogen shrugged, "Did they deserve to know anyway? I hope you find your answers about your sister I truly do. But now gal, get the tat. And get on with mine!" She jested.

"You know Imogen, maybe I will. Maybe I will."

She got to work on the slim thigh with caution. They chatted about work, their other friends and when she were finished and it were completed many hours later, she admired the piece with Imogen who was chuffed to pieces that she squealed.

"I love it. Thank you! From now on its miniskirts all the way so that I can show it off to all and sundry!" Imogen beamed cheekily.

Elfina looked at her friends admirable shapely legs that were much more slimmer then her own plump, rather knobbly ones. "You have the legs for it! I would!"

That she did.

"This tat will bring all the girls to the yard!" Crooned Imogen naughtily. Her and Elfina then sung together a nonsense song based on the song milkshake, that they had just then made up but with girls instead of the boys.

They laughed together like friends do. Elfina thought maybe that Imogen had the right idea at liking woman. For she had only had, had bad experiences with men. But the thought of being into a woman in that way she realised was not for her either.

Why couldn't she meet a handsome, alpha like man like in one of her favourite fantasy books? Like beauty and the beast but without the beast at the end of it? Like Twilight but without the sparkling and being hunted.

She couldn't.

Because she knew deep down that all that was simply fantasy, fiction. She herself had seen others in a deep kind of love, a deep companionship although she herself had never known it for her own. She had, had flings, the odd one-night stand and a relationship where he had sadly died after a clumsy night out had left in to him accidentally toppling into a river - drunk.

After a long while she had decided it was the time to try for love again, she had, had a few dates with - Karl but he had become – totally obsessed by her.

Speaking to her of his true love- her, texts, calls, bumping into randomly but not really, and when one day he had become too handsy and hit her and the police had done nothing – her word against his, she so had upped and left. Told few where she had gone. Her parents had died and surprisingly left her money in their will – a lot. She didn't even know they had that sort of money. They had never spent it on her.

A life of hand me downs, lack of spending.

But now it did not matter that she had got away - Karl were back. She did not want him or his fantasies, he would have to see that one day for himself. But would he?

She did not have the support of no big, bulky scary ass relatives that could threaten him into going away - permanently.

Who could scare him down a dark out of the way alley way with a baseball bat in their hand into never coming back to darken her door with their face... again.

She saw her friend off as Imogen had the day of, she was going to the shops, she worked in a Barclays bank and as she was letting her out, Elfina bumped into the postman. He handed her a pile of letters and gave her idle chit chat about the surprisingly sunny weather for a change.

That were true. This were Norfolk after all. Known famously for its up and down forever changing weather.

She flicked through the letters quickly and glanced at the bold and bright clock on the wall. Thirty minutes until her next appointment. She only had two left as Imogen's was booked up for most of the day which it had taken.

Bills, bills, then – oh no!

It was his hand writing. Again. Already? A day later. Jeez Louise! She tore open the letter in a flash with a stumbling, shaking hand.

The brunette read the words in her mind with a pounding heart. Only having received a letter from him the day previously she hadn't expected another one to arrive already or if at all.

Two days in a row! Not good. Not good at all.

At least it wasn't hand delivered this time. The thought of him near her, in her presence, at her home, made her feel sick to the core.

She read the letter in all nervousness.

PLEASE, I NEED TO SPEAK TO YOU

KARL. I LOVE YOU XXX

Fuck him! He could fuck off! Even his letter were cringe!

She angrily got up and tore the letter into shreds and put the now many small pieces into the small nearby bin with a scowl. She didn't realise that the time had flown on by until the door to the shop opened with a ting tong of the bell, and her next customer appeared with a fatherly smile.

It were the customer from yesterday's father. A small gentleman in his late seventies, with short white hair and a stick.

He explained what he wanted her to create for him. But unlike his son the day previously who wanted a tat in his mums memory, that his ma would have adored, he wated a tat as his dear departed wife never liked them at all, never wanted him to have one while she were alive.

Did his son know this? Doubtful.

Elfina secretly didn't blame him for getting one now that he could. She knew how it felt to not be allowed to do something that you wanted so desperately to do as an adult. Her own parents had stifled her, tried to take control of her everyday life and when she had nearly broke free from their hold -Karl had stepped into the fold with a vengeance.

Locking on, not wanting to let go. He would have chained her to him if she could.

Nearly knocking her down like a row of dominos. Well let him try! She was done playing his games for she herself were the master of them.

She had to be.

Back to her shop. For that was what were important to her. She had seen all sorts of reasons for people to get memory tats though. She put her all into them whilst working, her blood, sweat and tears, her concentration, and she loved every minute of doing it.

Each and every one.

The only ones that she were not comfortable with doing were - the name ones. On more than one occasion she had had to ask a customer if they really actually wanted their lovers name etched permanently in ginormous bold letters onto their skin and they always said yes, yes, they did.

Seeing them often in the city much later on with new partners and wondering what they thought of their partners, exes name on their partners body.

She had tattooed every part of the body that were possible, seen everything, done everything. Nothing surprised her anymore. And she also did piercings, she had a few of her own.

She got to work on his tat, he seemed to chat at first but then he was lost in his own space. When she were finally finished, she asked him what he had thought of it. Did he like it? She hoped so she really did.

But then... he appeared to be asleep.

How could you sleep through that she wondered with unease trickling in and concern in her pit? He hadn't even had it numbed!

"Mr Thompson? Mr Thompson?"

She tapped him gently on the shoulder in case he were merely just sleeping and out of it somewhat. He did not have any medical concerns or so he had said, and he had filled out on the form that a customer was required to fill out before a tattoo.

He were frighteningly still though.

Too still.

Horror then hit her from her spine downwards as she checked him for evidence of breath.

Of life.

There was none.

Her own heart pounding she checked for a heartbeat on his chest. Please be one, please be one! She begged internally as she felt his pulse in more place then one. No, she screamed it!

None.

He were dead! She had killed him! She ran across the room in a flustered flash as she realised, he was dying or likely already gone and she put her phone onto speaker.

999.

Whilst on the phone for an ambulance she pushed the chair that he was on down all the way so that he was lying flat down on it, luckily the chair did that or else she would have to have hoisted him up and onto the floor and she wasn't sure that she could lift a grown man up on her own.

She started to do chest compressions as she spoke to the operator who told her what to do each step of the way.

After five minutes of nothing she thankfully heard the sound of sirens and two ambulance men barged in, so she anxiously hung up the phone because help had arrived.

They took over whilst she paced the small shop nervously now her work there was done.

It wasn't looking good. No breath was coming. His skin was white like snow white, and his lips tinged blue.

Just then as they were getting him ready to go into the awaiting ambulance, she heard it.

Singing.

Beautiful, glorious singing like something an angel would sing if they so existed. She believed in them, believed in something, for there had to be something out there after living in that cruel world.

She then felt what resembled a small, petite hand on her shoulder, and she went from frazzled, in a state, to calm, peaceful.

At ease. All the anger, hate, fear left her body. Replaced by – joy. Which was wrong at a time like that!

"Is that you?" She whispered quietly.

Could it be her, could it really be her? But how? Did that mean she were...her sister were...dead.

"Can you hear singing?" She turned and asked one of the frazzled ambulance men who had stopped working on her poor departed customer as the sound of blissful singing got louder and louder.

And louder forever more.

Almost too loud for her mind to take while her heart beat fast from the fear of her customers death. But she did not want it to stop.

Not ever. Because that might mean she might not hear her voice again.

He smiled politely, "Yes love. Eerily beautiful at a time like this don't you think? Your next-door neighbour or whoever she is must have a good voice." He said as they covered the poor man up with a sheet.

Because it was clearly not kiss radio playing that tune. But someone live...

But it wasn't one of the neighbours with a sweet, angelic, melodic voice and she knew that. She would know that voice anywhere, had heard it sing many times before even if she had not had the privilege to have heard it in a long, long while.

Five years ago, or so.

She ached inside now.

This was after her poor customer being declared dead and then a simple sheet put over him so that he could go out to the ambulance respectfully. At least she had finished the tat on him she thought, and that he had gone out with a bang just like he would have wanted to have.

But she felt guilty though.

Guilt that he had died in her shop. Her place of work. Guilt that she hadn't been able to bring him back from the dead so as to spend more time with his only son who had now not just lost his mother but his father too.

She would have to give him a call, it were the least that she should do she thought as she paced and paced.

She saw the heroic ambulance men both off as they took the stretcher carefully out through the narrow door.

The singing still continued on; the audience remained unchanged.

"Is that you?" She said again in a startled whisper. Was it?

Nothing.

She soon felt what was much like a whisp of breath at her neck like a stolen kiss, and the beautiful singing to her sadness stopped suddenly. Something then squeezed her hand as though an invisible hand had reached out and touched hers with it.

"Ruby?" She spoke with tears glistening in her eyes. Who else could it be? There was no other explanation for it, or else she were going mad right about then.

But she knew she wasn't.

This wasn't the first time that she had sensed her sisters near presence by her, although it were the first time that she thought that she heard her sing just to her.

Whatever was touching her hand then left, left her alone, then next the shop door seemed to spookily open on its own and within seconds she heard the sound of fluttering, almost like it were the sound of wings and the peace that had coursed through her body, that anchored her, then left her soul as it rose from out of the ground.

Before the noise she thought she heard her sisters voice in a whisper – "Why can't you see me...."

Oh, but she so had desperately wanted to.

CHAPTER FOUR

I<u>DEN</u>
Ruby pounded hard on her sires door like she were in the mafia, at the end of the day. Iden answered in a crumpled fluster when she was just turning to leave for her own one.

To give up and go home.

Assuming that no one were home because he usually answered her really quickly with either a friendly warm greeting, or else a – 'what the fuck do you want Ruby?' and an indiscreet eye roll that he didn't bother to hide from her!

Obviously depending on his mood in question that day was how he reacted.

"Rube`s, I am kinda busy right now." Iden said in a dodgy flustered manner that meant he was up to something when he appeared at the door.

He now stood in the way of the large door with a large shoulder blocking her entry, and he did not invite her in like he normally begrudgingly would do. No eye roll to mention of either but a lowered gaze that meant he did not want to confide in her but what it were that he were up to.

She could see at a glance up and down swiftly that he was only wearing a tight pair of boxers, and his chest was bare, showing of his strange blotchy tattoo that was there proud as punch on his firm chest. Not something that she wanted to see, no, but she needed him then and there.

She had no one else she could turn to right then. To confide in. Except her posh friend Barren, her partner in crime, and he was on nights from now on in.

He preferred them.

Plus, someone had to be. People didn't just drop dead in the daytime, did they?! Although that would be quite darn well handy if they did so! She herself had never warmed to Ash. From what Iden had said it had taken him many years to open up to him and to give it time for them to bond if they ever did. She had only known them all five years, so they had all had many more years to bond, so else she had a bit of a wait there!

Maybe she should make some new friends in the realm?

But it were different in the realm then down there on earth. More different then she had thought that it would actually be in reality. No one met for a coffee, a date or visited the cinema downstairs to watch a movie. The only socialising that they did was round each other's homes, or at the clan headquarters.

Most of the clan had been there a lot, lot longer then she. In fact, she could say she was one of the youngest members of the blood taster, surviving group. It was lucky that she had not long had some vital blood or else that whole and entire conversation with her sire would have gone a whole different way!

"What kind of busy?" Ruby tetchily tried peering her head around the door of the home to see what he were then up to.

For Iden were acting suspicious.

was usually an open book and told everyone his business.

Iden`s gaze darkened and if she did not know him so well, she would feel at unease and want to run away, "Nothing to trouble you with Ruby. Its fine. Can we talk tomorrow though? I was in the middle of... some stuff."

Stuff. What stuff?

He said it in an almost rush as though he had somewhere better to be then with her at the door. Someone better to see. She hoped he wasn't having one of his orgy`s again!

Walking in on that she thought she had accidently entered an amateur porn shooting; it was why she usually now knocked and did not even bother to try the door knob.

Yep, he were up to something. No orgy going on but something else entirely that he were trying to keep hidden.

His usually slicked and kept proper, tidied hair was also messy as fuck to look at. His eyes were looking tired, and dark eyed like he had been up all... Oh no! She suddenly thought as a crazy thought hit her.

Not now. No, no, no, no!

Not when she had something for him. Something that she knew would make his whole entire world go into a crazy spin and turn it onto its axis and back again.

She gazed up at him stubbornly with stubborn eyes.

She were short yes, yes, she were, and it had always been an issue until she transformed into the living dead, but short as she were he was at least half a foot taller than a usual human man if not more, so he towered clearly over her.

Like a tall protective big brother. For that was all that he would be to her. Even if she were straight which she most certainly were not he would still be like a brother.

Plus, he was made for someone else. And so was she...

She needed to make him see the importance of what she came there for that day. She had flown so quick just to get there. If not for him, then for her.

And for- Elfina. The one that really mattered in all this.

She grabbed his arm hard, "It's important Iden. But it can wait if you want. But as I say again it is important," She let go of his thick arm and turned to leave his home with a sulky look upon her face.

Hoping that he would ask her to stay so she did not have to go away back to the loneliness of her own home with this revelation playing firmly on her mind. Because if he didn't, didn't ask her in, she might have to go back down to the human world to see her awesome, beloved sister again and to just hold her.

To sing for her.

To wish that she could see her – even just a glimpse. For being invisible to ones sibling, ones work place, ones friends and colleagues – well it really sucked.

We all want to be known and not to be ignored.

She doubted that he cared for that idea of her going down to earth though even for just a fleeting trip. If she did, he would have to scold her, punish her if he found out about it. To lead an example of her to the rest of the clan.

She wanted to sing so bad right then but knew that might look-crazy. She loved fucking singing, especially when she were so bloody stressed out that she just wanted to open her mouth and let it all out...

Singing in the shower, singing in the rain, although the weather was usually neutral in their realm and hardly did anything but just be there.

Who didn't love singing? Once a song that she loved got into her head, then there was no stopping her. Heck she even had karaoke at her home of five years. Her and Barren could sing one heck of a tune together and apart.

Would have it at every home that she visited if she could do, and they wanted it. But Iden`s ideas of parties and hers were not the one and the same.

But she hadn't meant to sing in front of Elfina earlier that day or in her near ear shot it had just shot out of her in her pain at bumping into her.

She hadn't realised that she were even there at first entering the shop. Not even noticing the shop was named simply - Elfina`s. Too caught up in her own vital soul work, still young enough to worry all the time about making a simple mistake when collecting, but old enough to talk sense in to herself so that it all went, usually smoothly.

The soul for collection was their main focus on entering the human`s domain. Should be their only focus when they went down there to where the humans lived for a time.

But it hadn't of been. Of course, she had seen the old man off in the respect that he had deserved to have been seen in. But there had been more to it. More that she had found out on collecting him...More that she had discovered on leaving there for here.

"Wait." She swung round at his stern commanding voice.

Iden grabbed her arm gently with a hand for he would never hurt her, not if he so could help it anyway.

"I will just see my guest off, its fine Ruby. Promise. I will be there if need be." He reassured her with a small smile. Although happy about it was another thing. He was pissed off – that she knew.

See who off? Guest? Sex partner? She wondered. Wasn't really any of her business was it.

"No, no. I..." She stuttered.

Ruby soon had her answer to that as a usually well-groomed, immaculate, luscious blonde Justina, came out and stood glaring from behind Iden like an over- bearing rottweiler with sharp vicious teeth to match. Looking like she had got dressed in the dark, so it was clear as day to anyone with a gaze that she had just pulled her clothes on so quickly as to come to the door behind her obvious current sex partner right then.

"Oh god."

Ruby muttered this under her breath. She had seen the two together before, he was their leader of course she saw him with various woman and it was not unusual for woman to be traipsing all over him like he were sex itself, but she thought that he would not sink as low as that one that he were currently having a taste of.

The lowest of the low.

Justina. Even hearing her name mentioned in passing made Ruby feel grossed out and uncomfortable because they were two completely different people.

She had hoped that she would trip up, not do her work, get banished or put down by those above. But Justina was one of the ones who skirted around, did her earth duties in a basic enough way as though not to get punished for the lack of empathy that she dealt out with her work.

"It`s fine, get back to urm... whatever it was that you were both doing."

Ruby emphasised the 'doing.' She did not like to think what that quite were without wanting to puke in her own mouth. The idea of Iden and that thing behind him fornicating as one made her want to bleach her eyes out with bleach, bleach and yep – more bleach besides!

A shopful would do.

He needed better taste.

Soon he would have it if he listened.

The blonde z list wannabe was evidently not happy at the interruption because she wiped down her clothing and sneered back to the smaller then her female,

"Me. He was doing me." Justina sneered this with venom in her eyes, pouting in disgust with vicious painted purple lips as she saw who it was actually interrupting her evening of slip n slidey fun with the local hot clan leader that she wanted as her vampire groom.

Iden was hers, she would be the clan leaders mate.

She would see to that! Justina just by looking at her mad as hell body language wasn't letting the little scrote at the door – Ruby or whatever she called herself, get in the way of her achieving that!

Justina had been turned into a vampire by an ex-member of their clan – Fess, ten years previously. One who had only seemingly turned juicy, hot females, as he liked to call it that resembled super models. It had turned out that not all of them were dying when he first met them either or even a step near. He had not been long turned when he became banished either. Because he would never toe the line.

Where he had gone no one knew, for he had not been seen again. Iden liked to think that he had been happily decapitated or burnt, one could only hope so. He doubted that he would be so lucky as to know that Fess had gone through that fate.

You see, you could only turn someone into a vampire that was at deaths peak, by drinking their so delicious blood, then giving them your vampire blood for them to recuperate.

This would cause their heart to gradually stop and then the transformation into a vampire was soon to begin a short time later. The stuff of fantasy`s.

But Fess had not been aware of this.

He had not thought to ask anyone, or he did not even have the brain cell to and had just acted on his own stupid impulse.

Those that were full of life at attempted transformation just, well they simply died – and they did not come back at all. Justina was one of this so-called super model like hotties that Fess had turned and who had luckily for her survived the ordeal.

The black curly haired Fess was apparently according to him hoping for a house full of ever obeying, gorgeous woman on their knees for him, available for his every command, his every wish. His every want

But instead- they all got up on their two feet and a pair of new growing wings and went their own way from then on in. Fess was bitter that he had died, bitter that he had left someone he truly cared about more than anyone else in the world so for this he went on a bad, vamp changing rampage.

The one`s he turned- left without him.

And Iden kicked him clean out of the clan when he found out that this Fess, this newbie vamp, was turning the healthy humans into - one of them.

But killing them off in the process more than like.

That was a firm no, no in their world. They did not do that there. Ever.

His clan member had thought that they were doing him a favour turning him as he laid dying in a car crash. Little did they know that he was wholly responsible for the whole crash. And in turning him they had unleashed a bitter monster that wanted to create others.

Iden knew that his own brother was the baddest vampire of all that he had ever known. But Fess was a close second.

"Lovely." Said Ruby in disgust at Justina`s comment, her face and nose scrunched up and she did not bother to disguise her unease. She could have slapped Iden for his lack of taste.

Iden sensed the tension unfolding, went to nudge Justina back inside his large home with a gentle prod, but she instead sprung out of the door with her usual hot-headed mind of her own like an unstable jack in the box.

"Get your own man." Justina pointed rudely at Ruby and her claws then grew all the more longer into sharp talons, her majestic face then turned into a horror- some vampire nightmare that would make even a strong human soil their clothes and run out of the room screaming.

She snarled in warning to Ruby to back off. But Ruby was not going anywhere. This were her friend; this was where she would stay.

"Justina." Iden warned her softly to start with. Giving her a chance to ease up and to obey his command.

She simply grunted.

Too lost in her own anger to think rationally and to make decisions with a clear mind.

The petite woman though were no bodies pushover, "Its fine Iden. I can handle this thing. Justina, In the years that I have been here in this realm, if you really haven't even noticed that I prefer the cunt over the cock," Ruby hollered at the blonde cow getting in her way of much needed support and advice from her sire right then.

Getting in her face with a gruesome smug look.

Getting in the way of what she wanted to say so desperately to her sire, her friend, "Then you are more stupid then I presumed you to be."

The blonde vampire slapper shuddered and grimaced openly at the small other female who she obviously had not realised- fancied chicks. "That's even more sickening then girl. That you are not after my man but are yet after me. You people make me sick." Justina spat out vilely.

A blatant homophobe as well as a bitch then it so seemed.

Ruby had dealt with far worse when back on earth in terms of peoples stupidity and prejudices so was not fazed.

This bitch here was simply nothing.

The petite brunette, half the size of the shrieking vixen on the doorstep but with double the heart, rolled her eyes clear to the sky, "Umm, yeah ok, no thanks. I said I prefer cunt; it still doesn't mean I want your old crusty one love. I`ll pass if you please."

This went down as well as a sack of shit, "Why you! You would be lucky to have me and my fantastic fanny. Lucky, I tell you! Lucky!" Justina sped out off of the doorstep and made to hit Ruby in the face hard, her clawed finger fist lay clenched, but Iden got in the way of them both as he sped speedily into the way of the two-vamp woman in just his bare tight shorts.

He grew so tall and so darn fierce and much like the clan leader that they all love but respected and who they would at times – solely fear.

He made the rules, so they had to stick with them and now as she pulled back in alarm, Justina was under no further qualms that if she even so touched little Ruby, touched even a single brown hair on her delicate little head that she would die that very day at the hands of her own lover.

And it was now clear that he would not shed a single tear for his sex partner or that he would regret a single action. Justina had known that he had a bond with the bratty small woman as she saw the two together.

But she did not realise how deep the bond lay.

"No!" He shouted angrily to Justina like a demon possessed. His claws descended and grabbed her arm.

No one would touch her he hissed! He had always been so protective of his dear little friend that he had created, that he had saved from a beating and much more. No one quite knew why he felt so close to her, nor did he.

But he did.

They soon would though...The answer was nearing and coming closer with each second of the clock.

Justina stood down from the one manned fight with a fearful, defiant scowl on her blonde brows, but her sharp thin face showed that she was unhappy too. She seethed with held in frustration that looked like it took every inch of her being not to over flow and unleash again at the petite woman who although she had outed herself as a lesbian, kept getting in her way.

And no one got in Justina's way...

Iden would not banish her, not for that, but she had to go away for a short time while things cooled down and she learnt her lesson. Other vamps he noticed were watching from a far at the altercation happening on his own doorstep. Like a live episode of Neighbours until it got sadly dropped after many years of course...

"Do not come here until you apologise, until you think about what you have done. You are lucky you are walking away intact." Iden ordered the stubbornest member of the clan.

Who sadly were probably the sexiest.

Justina winced at his words. She had never made him mad like this before and she feared that it would be final. He usually liked her dominant nature; most were afraid to show their dominance over the clan leader that they knew so well.

And most would not dare to...

"Iden I am sorry." The tall, willowy blonde, clinging to him and he nudged her away uncaringly like she were nothing. The beautiful one that he had not long been pounding hard with his cock from behind said.

Iden felt slight remorse at letting Justina seduce him again and again. The fact that he had her love bites messily all over his neck and she had then nearly hit his dear friend who was half her size whilst in her temper, showed that he had put his sexual appetites before what he should have put first.

His friends, his job, and his duty to the clan. But he would not appear weak. He would not apologise to anyone.

"You, leave." He pointed at the woman who had been just warming his bed. Warming his thick cock.

"And you in here. It better be important." He rolled his eyes at Ruby. And... he were back.

Ruby went to follow. Justina faltered.

"I`m not banished, am I? You can't tar me with the same brush as Fess..."

It seemed even the hard heart Justina had a heart in there somewhere.

His face briefly softened at her plight but then it hardened. "Don't be wet Justina. No. Just go home. We will talk another day. It was supposed to be a sex session not an episode of Jeremy Kyle."

Yes, even vampires like Jeremy Kyle! Iden did. It made his life look great.

He slammed the door hard in Justina`s face before she could say anything else with those thick lips of hers. She had to step back from the door to avoid impact with her face.

"Call me!" He heard her say as the door slammed to. Not a bloody chance in this version of hell that he felt he were currently residing in would it be any time soon!

"Come." He gestured and lead Ruby through to the large lounge and she meekly followed.

"I`m sorry." Ruby said. Yeah, it seemed like they all were that day, he groaned internally to himself! Wishing sometimes that his house on the realm was on a deserted island somewhere instead of smack bang in the middle of his clans homes.

Where they could seek him out.

He was curious though about what led Ruby there to his door that day. Something was bugging her, and it must be important for her not to just up and leave and come back until his rutting were gone and done. He just hoped that whatever it were that had brought her there that it was important enough to make him lose a night of great ass sex and for his latest fling to cause a ruckus in the street where all and sundry could watch.

For Justina might be a blonde, beautiful psychopathic, clingy, and moronic at times, but she honestly was a good lay and quite intelligent. And normally discrete about who`s pants she were currently pulling down that very evening.

Sometimes the vampires amongst them gossiped even worse than the human local rags did, and he knew that it would be only a matter of time before the whole clan knew that he had been doing Justina and that she had stormed off into the night because something had come up.

It didn't help that vampires had amazing hearing either...

"What did you want to tell me?" He asked raising a curious brow in question at his smaller friend.

She shocked him as she eyed him, "I saw my sister earlier. Today in fact."

A statement that he was not expecting to hear from her. Because she should not have been visiting her only sibling down on earth where the humans lived, and she knew it. He had forbade it. It was one of his rules.

He looked in the mirror and sorted out his hair as he grimaced.

Yes, vampires did have reflections! It would be crazy if they did not. Plus, he were - vain. Who wouldn't be if they looked like him?

He sighed, "I thought we went through this. Was you not soul collecting today? You can't be doing this Ruby! It's against the rules!"

For it were. They all must abide by them.

"Sod the rules!" She said it like a reluctant teen having a bratty tantrum. "But I did. I promise you."

"Did you?" He yelled out clearly exasperated and flung his hands out in his ever-growing manic despair.

She glared at her sullen sire, "Yes, yes of course I did!" She after all took her soul collection duties extremely seriously. She had promised that she would once he had changed her, made a vow even to her sire and what not.

What did he take her for?

A bloody muppet, she wondered! She tried to explain this to her sire without losing her cool at him. He needed to know the truth. His own one.

But he was being his usual stubborn self and in this only his own view was the right one that there were.

Ruby shot out, "Iden, I saw my sister when I was collecting a soul. Not off watching flipping Mario movie! Even though I am jarred off that you said no, we couldn't go. I stand by that. The souls body who I collected; he died in her shop suddenly it is why I saw her. By accident."

Iden sped over and reached out a larger then her own one hand and clasped her shaking one.

"Jeez I am sorry Rubes. I am also sorry for doubting you. I should never have. I trust you." He sighed. Stunning even himself with his first ever apology that he knew of.

"Do you though?"

She questioned him this as only a friend and not as a clan leader. She would leave the clan way, way before she ever stopped being his friend even though at times, he did not deserve her to be.

But she owed him so much. Without him she would have just been another victim to those filthy men. Without him she would have taken her last quaking breath whilst the scumbag men who had done it had wondered free, and with no unease.

Now she knew they were where they deserved- the lower realm, where they would spend all of eternity fighting their battles.

Or hell if you like to call it.

There in the lower realm they would make her justice that she had dished out with her sire`s help look like simply child's play.

On and on and on.

He did not need to think, even for a moment about whether he did or not but simply - "I do. Absolutely! Drink? Sadly, I think that there is no alcohol here though quite just yet. It is on my to do list along with bringing more blood in for storage." Quite why he had let stocks slide remained a mystery that only he would know the answer to.

"No thanks. Iden. You need to keep stores going. Look what happened to you yesterday. You nearly looked crazed!" Her eyes widened at the memory of it.

For he had.

She did not need to tell him for that he knew, he had felt the change in him unleash, "I know."

"What would you have done to poor ol Geoffrey if he hadn't have gave you that vial of blood?" She pondered out loud licking her lips. Clearly thirsty herself.

"Probably would have eaten him alive." He chuckled, not funnily.

Her gaze narrowed at his cold-hearted words, "Nice. There is something else that I wanted to tell you. But the idea of it is surreal that it feels like a dream to me more then you could believe. Also telling you what I have to when you are wearing that tramps bites all on your neck, I must admit it makes me feel really uncomfortable in doing so." She shuffled on the spot awkwardly.

She reminded him of a deer caught in headlights.

He frowned. "Why? It is nothing that you have not seen before is it not? You must know by now that I like a dominant woman in the bedroom as I like to dominate it from outside. Happen we have not had a bitch about woman together of late. We must soon. Or are you still playing it cool?"

"Don't, just don't." Ruby looked like she wanted to chuck up her guts at that notion right there and then.

Iden tended to overshare with them all in all his exploits. Which was what he were doing now.

Oversharing.

She had been on a few dates herself since being made a permanent member of the vampire realm of course she had being so eternity made her slightly horny.

As it did them all.

But now she knew of having a human mate she said it, made her feel almost like she would be cheating on someone who were faceless but still the most important thing to her.

But that one day she would forever know.

She had not gone the whole way with a woman as of yet although she had wanted to so darn bad. Oh, how she had! But she had decided to stick to what was before and to instead wait for the rest.

She had all the time in the world to.

"Ok I won't." He teased. "But you will miss out on my sordid tales like such as when Justina stuck a really large cucumber..."

Ruby quickly interrupted what she knew she did not want to hear out of his lips and put her small hands over her ears, "Promise me that you will not finish that sentence or mention your sex life again to me. Unless you can find me a vampire therapist anywhere that is. Do you know of any?"

She chuckled half-heartedly of the idea of it.

Most the vamps did not bother with their old occupations, yes, they had their hobbies as eternity were a long time to spend their spare time doing nothing.

But whilst soul collecting, living their heartbeat free, infinity lives then there was not much time for other things. Plus, they had free houses, endless supply of food and usually blood on tap, then they did not need much else. They could have the outfits that they wanted plus he knew that some often stole from the earth shops when they required something extra.

But did not admit it to him.

Well why not when they could traipse through the malls unseen but only heard. And couple that with being able to take without being seen on human CCTV.

Tempting.

"I will try then." He said rather sweetly although she knew that he likely wouldn't.

She studied him deeply with a curious gaze.

Would he think her mad, she wondered with what was to come next?

Maybe. But it was time to bite the crimson bullet and tell him.

She looked up at her strange sire and asked suddenly, "Have you ever heard of vamps with shall we say... extra powers?" She paused.

He looked intrigued by her question, took a cool coke out the fridge, pulled open the tab and chugged it down nearly in one.

"Why the questions?"

"Please just answer. Then all will be revealed."

"Well, we all have super speed, fast healing, enhanced eyesight, hearing and a magnificent sense of smell and taste. But I don't need to tell you about this Ruby for obviously you already know."

Listing what they could do. Like a vampire book for dummies. But Ruby was not one. Why did she want or need to know of this?

She nodded at his listing of traits with a beyond serious face, "Apart from that I mean."

Why didn't he get her she thought to herself? What would it take to get it through to him what she actually meant? Would she have to draw a picture here?

He put his chin in his hand and thought hard in concentration. He knew something bad was about to hit him, there was no other explanation for this crazy conversation that they were currently both having about powers that she should already know of.

Being as she, herself had them.

They all did.

He continued on, "Well, we have some powers, the mild magic, so that we can give the soul slight extra time in case we want to transform them into one of us. We can zap them up new clothes if they are naked on death. Tidy them up a bit. That's about it...What's this about? Have you discovered something? What is it?" He urged her.

No, he pleaded of her.

She had indeed found out something. He would not know what had hit him. He would not be prepared.

He waited in earnest.

"Ruby, is everything ok?" He seemed concerned by her hesitation. He knew her, so knew when she were troubled.

He expected many, many things to leave her lips. But what she said next left him as speechless as a mime.

"My sister is your mate. I think so anyway."

There she had said it out loud without no hesitation. Ok, maybe some.... How would he take it?

Iden in all his dark-haired glory simply stood there gawking at her in a long and stunned cold silence. The strong clan leader now well appearing for a time to resemble a nervous boy with a nervous gait.

He lowered his strong face and bit his lip anxiously.

He then composed himself, threw his empty coke down hard, hurriedly grabbed a basic grey Nike top from the messy pile in his room. (Hey, vamps like looking cool too!) One that she noted covered his bites which were like he had said, already fading fast as though they were never there.

And he threw on a pair of black loose combats to go with and simple striped ankle socks. Not quite caring that there was someone else there in the room, he would get dressed either way.

Unluckily enough for her she had seen it all before. But even the sight of his ginormous almost dripping pecker and oh so sweet hanging hairy ass balls could not sadly make a girl want what she did not already.

"How do you know of this?" His eyes then blazed like burning fire into hers, searching for some answers that he needed. Hope filled him then urgent worry.

Any ones.

Did she have them? He needed them. He wanted them so bad that he could pull them out from her, and he would hold so desperately on so fucking tightly that it would hurt every muscle in his body to. He held his breath tight in anticipation, because he felt like he was hallucinating or dreaming, or dying, and then waited.

Not like he needed to breathe anyway, for it was purely from habit that he did so. Because he felt like if he stopped that he would be dead-dead. Even though that were simply not true.

Ruby was now in a slight panic that maybe she should have kept her mouth shut tightly. Or else waited until a better time for it. But secrets like that could not be kept for long for they would hurt those who did not deserve it to the most.

Ruby tried to explain in simple terms.

"My sister. She smelt of...She smelt of you Iden. That whisky that you so love. That musk that you spray all over yourself and have to inflict on us. But that's not just it. The shop, her shop. In the air it smelt so faintly like me too. Like I had sprayed my own scent all over the place. Which I could not as I am of course – the walking dead." She paused then continued.

"My mate knows her. She must know my sister! She must be in her circle, in her midst! In her life! But how does she? I never should have left there for here. I should have survived somehow." She shook her head in her sweet sorrow.

"You did survive. You are here with me now."

"You know what I mean."

"YOU. DID. SURVIVE. RUBY." He said in almost a roaring shout to her. Because in his mind she did. "Your sister. Wow. It's a small world after all." He beamed like he had just been given a free lifetime of takeaway pizzas filled to the brim with sizzling onions, spicy peppers and endless pepperoni on top.

Could it be true?

Maybe Ruby had lost the plot? Maybe she was without blood and now beginning to go feral from it... But he could not put her down. Nor could he watch it if it happened.

His mind was in an over spin now.

But as he stood there and thought - It all made fucking sense now to him that he felt like a moron that he hadn't worked it all out so much earlier. The pull that he had, had all along to his dear little friend Ruby. The deep friendship that the two of them normally shared, and that had grown beautifully over a short amount of time into something - unique.

She were like his little sister. If his own sister wasn't dead, she had died many years ago. He had almost forgotten what she had looked like. But he would never forget her voice. That would remain in his memories forever.

Because it now appeared that little Ruby was – his fated mates, younger sister. But how did Ruby know of this? If she knew her own one and of others ones, then that was dangerous stuff right there and then. This particular info could fall into the wrong hands.

Many vamps would want her, she was the key to their puzzle.

And with that the life that he led had just handed him a miracle, had also handed him a curse. For the door to his home, his own personal sanctuary and retreat flew open.

A lone dark-haired figure stood there stalking in the now dark doorway. A figure that Iden well knew, one that had gave him the gift of immortality, the chance of redemption.

Had pulled him up from the broken heap where he lay at the scene of his death.

But the figure there lurking was also – a out and out psycho.

It spoke first. Its voice a dark whisper. "Evening all."

"Rhys." He gritted his teeth at seeing his brother again. Knowing that the pleasantries from his brother were fake as could be.

"Hello Iden." His brother grinned back with a cruel unimpressed smile that lingered. Even the air felt polluted with his scent entwined in to it. It didn't smell rotten or bad, just he was the bad one, He had spent too long in the darkness that had taken over a small part of the realm.

Would he ever get out of there? Doubtful because his brother had been there nearly as long as what he had been in the good part of the realm...

Rhys was much like his younger brother were. But while Iden was a leader, he was also a friend to his people the majority of the time when he were caught in a good mood.

Rhys only know how to lead the bad. He did not know what true friendship actually were or loyalty. For him there was no redemption arc.

Iden himself had slicked back hair. Rhys however had longer hair that were now tied up and a more wicked dark and dishevelled look to his person.

Donning leather trousers, gloves and a ripped top that showed off his obvious six pack. The darkness clan leader would make woman swoon if they did not know the danger that followed him everywhere he went like the shadows that stalked the night.

The two hoped that he would not stop here for long so as the whole and entire realm did not get polluted with his crippling madness.

"I thought I smelt something bad." Iden grimaced on seeing his sibling again after so long. Not wanting to turn his back from his brother- in case he stabbed him in it. He would not put it past him - he had tried it before.

He had given him eternal life, he bet that it was he that finished it.

Iden mentioned the ginormous elephant in the room that filled it up, spat it out, "What do you want Rhys? Why have you come here?" He gestured round his amazing home. His brothers he guessed would be just as big.

He did not know for there was no way that he would venture there.

Rhys at this question turned speedily around wide eyed, almost manic with anger that would not yield, and then simply pointed at Ruby with a finger with an eery chill that crept through the two friends like a holiday at the north pole.

"I came here to ask you to join the darkness cause with me my little brother, once again." The elder one said wickedly as he pinched his brothers cheek firmly with a clawed grip which was quickly slapped away from his face so that he could not mark it.

Iden simply rolled his eyes.

They had been here before, "You know the answer, it was the same as the last time that you asked me. The same as before. I have company so now is not the time for this." He nodded towards Ruby who avoided the bad ones stare by hiding out of harms reach.

Rhys was not deterred, "I thought that maybe after giving you time to think, years to think, that you might have – reconsidered it by now."

"I would rather give up my work and go live in the lower realm then ever join your terrible cause." Iden spat out.

This he would.

"You don't know what you are missing." The elder brother sneered. Iden eyed him, "Oh but I do."

Rhys sniffed into the air as a mesmerising scent wafted into his fine nose and he then realised that they were not alone in the large room built for many. He speedily left his younger brothers side in a flash and walked over to a frazzled Ruby, who could not take her eyes off of the scary lord of the darkness.

She shivered. How could these two actually be brothers she wondered? Most people did. Iden had been turned by him, he had told her his story of how he were created. He had no shame in it. But it was for no good reason. No good reason at all that he were now head of an invisible clan of vampires in a secret realm rather than long buried in a cemetery at the edge of some town.

"Hmm. What is this?" The darkness clan leader stepped forward then leant forwards towards the smaller Ruby who flinched openly at his touch, she shuddered, making him laugh bluntly. "What do we have here? Hello my pretty! Oh? Her, I want her. This one. My mate. You have been keeping her from me it so seems my brother."

Oh.

The penny dropped for Iden. He realised that his elder kin must feel the same strange but glorious pull to the small brunette, that Iden had always felt somewhere in his core. Maybe his brother had even smelled his mate on her also? Though who knows who that could be...

If Ruby could sense that her sister was apparently his fated one and that she knew briefly of her own fated, then maybe Rhys's poor unfortunate for her mate, was closer than one realised also.

The brothers began to fight in an array of clouding violence. Iden outraged at Rubys behalf and Rhys outraged at thinking that his brother had betrayed him.

"She's not for you, she's someone else's." The vamp of the light said dangerously.

"She is not yours either!" The one of the dark roared wildly.

"No. But she is not yours either big brother." Iden repeated.

The fight continued on with punches thrown, claws ripping out.

But while Iden was the best shot, his brother was the darkness, the darkness himself who had come to the door with spite, anger and rage thrown in.

He made the darkness into his own shape, its own style, and he moulded it in to what he wanted it to become.

So, Rhys had the upper hand.

Always. The two brothers duelled on through time, finally frightfully reunited again, while the small built female looked on in startled horror where she did not want to get in the way as Iden's home was trashed by the two figures knocking into everything.

The rage that they both felt for each other appearing, unleashing, unwavering...

Looking open mouthed in complete amazement at the scene before her, but at also that this handsome beast who she had never met, was under the false reasoning that they were entwined.

Never! Kill her now...

Iden became over run by the power that his brother held so eventually fell to the floor with a gasp, a hand stretched out as he tried to stay up, struggling to get up as something while he lay pinned down under his brother, as he had then sharply sprayed him straight in the face with cold- hearted malice.

"What the! You dirty dog! Fight like a real man." Iden raised a shaky fist at the older one who had dared to disturb their peace. The celebration of finding his mate...

"No brother, I would rather fight like this thanks. It's somewhat quicker."

Rhys had grabbed Ruby in a lock hold as his brother who had got up again fell hard from the strange spray. She squirmed in his thick arms as he tried to hold her, and the dark one then slapped her hard across the face with a loud guiltless clang.

"Shut up!" He hissed. His face going and staying murderous. "Leave her alone!"

"I`m not your mate, I'm a lesbian, you bloody idiot!" She tried biting her captor which sadly for her- he seemed to like so she tried to kick him in the privates, but the fearsome one had some sort of weird spray that he sprayed in her face with a never-ending chill.

It must have been what he used on Iden she realised wondering why he would not get up and help his friend!

He always helped her. So why not now?

It made her so sleepy. It were horrible.

She tried to fight the groggy feeling that tore through her, but it were no good.

The stranger held her tight, giving her flashbacks from being held down that night five years back. She screamed and shouted, flailed, and she tried opening her miraculous white wings to block him out from taking her, but they seemed trapped inside her.

What was holding them? She panicked.

"She doesn't like being held down. Give her some room you are making her panic!" Iden yelled at seeing Ruby in distress in his own brothers arms.

He could not get up and take the panic for his own.

Rhys bad as he were, let up but also still hold on to the girl – but lighter.

The bigger man pulled her roughly towards the door and as Iden came too and tried to save her with all of his might, Rhys leaned over and sprayed him again too with the weird knock out spray.

Was that even a thing? It must be because here they were both the friends struggling to stay awake and to fight.

As his world started to go crazily dark again, Iden cried out to his surrogate sister with a question, and with hope, "I will come for you Ruby, don't worry. What is her name? I will find her. Then she will be the saviour of us both. That I am sure of."

He needed to know it.

Hear it whispered straight from her mouth.

He needed to find his connected love, the one that he had waited many moons for and then save his small, friend from his brothers cruel clutches. He wasn't sure what way round to do it.

If his elder brother thought she was his mate, he wondered then why did he slap her? For even the leader of the darkness should treasure their mate like the precious gem that they were as if they were their whole entire world from then on in.

Because they were.

A mate was... it was everything.

"Elfina. Her name is Elfina! Help me Iden! Bloody get off man!" Ruby screamed in anger as Rhys for some reason then bit down hard into her wrist with his vicious fangs. Sucking on her purple- ish vampire blood. Trying to mark her for his own, with his own scent.

Make her his dark eternal bride of the realm.

Not quite realising that she weren`t. She was not his mate to have- but someone else's entirely.

"You have my word, Ruby. Rhys, I will come for you, and it won't be pretty!"

The next thing that Iden knew was, was the world going black - and it sucked him down into it.

CHAPTER FIVE

E LFINA
Elfina sat in the local bar nearest to her flat and shop where she had been for hanging out for the past hour – The cleft, with her group of usual friends. After the day that she had had she needed to unwind, to relax. To talk.

It was not too busy in the bar and not too quiet- a perfect match if she did say so. The music was r n b. From now and from the old days.

Imogen was there also on one of the fabric bright sofas wearing a black leather clingy skirt, that showed off her new rainbow tat that must have still smarted, the one that she already loved so much.

And had told everyone about.

The rainbow glistening with all the different colours. If she hadn't swore of girls, then likely Imogen would have been down the local gay bar to show it off to all that went there.

Or Elfina would have suspected her to of.

Megan was yet more casual in baby pink matching trackies whilst Elfina had gone for a flowery sleeveless shirt and jeans.

Lovella was in dark denim, bootcut jeans and a green vest which showed off her really large bosom, with her black hair loose for a change.

It was one of those places that you could wear anything that you wanted to.

Elfina had there quietly discussing quietly the events of earlier that day to her trusted three friends. She had shut the shop down early, then cancelled her last appointment as respect for the deceased customer.

But also, because she were too shaken up by things to keep on going with her work right then. She needed a clear head to ink, and it was not clear in the slightest.

But who wouldn't be shaken after that? Her elderly customer had died in one of her chairs. In her place of work.

She had then afterwards heard her actual sister, her presumed dead sister, actually singing a bloody song! It was surprising that she hadn't been admitted to a funny farm by now!

"I can't believe I heard my sister." A tear in her eye that threatened to shed. The thought had been going round and round all late afternoon in the lass`s mind.

Lovella leant forward her elbows on the table like the lady that everyone thought she was – but clearly wasn`t.

"Maybe my dear she is alive after all? Maybe that is why you heard her voice." Lovella did evidently not believe in the afterlife in the same way that Elfina herself did.

"Or maybe someone is playing tricks on you?" Butted in Megan.

Ever suspicious also. Slightly tipsy more than like. She could go from quiet to loud mouthed with no filter in one hour flat once she had been drinking nonstop.

Megan had said also that she wouldn't put it past that stalking rat who was obsessed with her friend to try to wind Elfina up more and more until she ran scared into his arms for help. Or so he thought.

Not happening. The friends wouldn't allow it to happen. Plus, Elfina wasn't stupid.

Much.

She was done with Karl. It had never been a thing anyway just a few crappy dates.

"Hmm that seems to be stretching it." Imogen added. She was in team Elfina in believing in the unknown that were out there.

Megan looked at the blonde in the group astounded, "Well what explanation is there?"

"If Elfina said she heard her sister maybe she did in fact hear her sister?"

"Hmm." Lovella was distracted herself and turned round and saw two men staring their way.

"Do you know the hotties?" She nudged Elfina who were a regular in there along with Megan. Sometimes they came in just the two of them on a quick lunch break for a chat.

And a bitch.

Ever the matchmaker Lovella was such a wide eyed romantic that she was like a readymade cupid. Elfina wondered at times where her bow were kept on her person. As long as she kept it away from her all was good.

"Who?" Elfina turned around now also distracted to where her friend was now looking at. Her eyes narrowed; her dark lipped smile warm. Not really wanting the distraction of guys to spoil their female chit chat.

Or to be pulled.

Two suited and booted guys were looking their way and not being discreet about it either from what they could tell.

"No, no I don't." She shrugged. "Holiday makers maybe?" They frequented the area, but they did look more like business men by the way they were suited and clutched their brief cases tightly in a curled grip.

Then she saw him. No, she felt him. Without touch. Only purely with mind. On the other side of the bar to where she were then.

There he were.

His eyes were shining dark blue, but more like speckled black. His jaw was firm and strong, his face and cheeks chiselled. Hair that were so dark and it were slicked back with not a single strand out of place from what she could see, that were a few shades darker then her own now styled up, so that it looked nice hair.

He wore a long dark leather coat with what appeared to be nothing underneath on his bare chest. She could see strange tats engraved on his arm that drew her gaze to them and a large unusual one on his chest in the centre like nothing that she had seen before.

Like him.

She gasped in complete and utter awe at him and his perfect soul that she wanted. Not ever seeing anyone quite like him.

Or wanting to again.

She shivered in desire as he looked her way, over at her curious stare or maybe he had from the start? She would never know.

She wondered how could she have not noticed such a fine specimen there in her local by himself? With no one else. Where was his drink for, he did not have one? What brought him there that was a mystery?

His arms were so massively thick and his shoulders so darn broad. His last item of clothing apart from his boots was tight, oh so tight trousers, that would have made most men look like they were trying too hard to impress.

He just looked like perfection himself. If he had his own calendar- she would have bought it. If he were leaving the county- she would want to follow him there so she could be nearer. Heck If he brought this bar that they were in – she would be in there every day.

Day or night.

The pull between them was so immense.

Unreal. She knew without reading him that it were more than mutual from the way he drew her in with his mysterious but penetrating glance.

She had sworn off of all men for good, yes, she had, and quite rightly so with everything that she had been though for no fault of her own. Wanting to stay safe, stay secure, as an ever-living spinster in her own protective bubble until her days on earth were then done, after all that she had entailed.

Now he had appeared to her, this... godlike creature, she wanted back in to the world of dating men fast, and she wanted it right then!

Damn you sexy man! She cursed internally as her own neglected coochie filled up with unashamed warmth and desire for the body parts that could possibly ever entertain it.

The thoughts of her dropping dead customer, off of her odd encounter with the mysterious kind, that her sister may have visited beyond the grave, the letter from a stalking deadbeat were now gone temporarily from her startled memory.

She barely could even remember her own name now that she was caught in a trap.

But darn it she wanted so bad to be caught. To be spanked.

She gasped in shock and so did he, as their eyes now locked together into a mysterious trance where neither one wanted to back up or to get away from the other.

Like she were being hypnotised. And he were the hypnotist who did it.

He looked shocked beyond belief at her very being there in front of him in that uneventful bar. Why was he so shocked?

Not realising it was because she could see him when no one else could there.

He were invisible to all earthbound – yet she could see him. Finally see him.

She came out of her love trance after a few more moments and nudged Imogen in disbelief for help pulling her out of her own trance. Gasping again in delight but disguising it as a cough- so that no one would know what she felt.

"Do you see that guy?" As Imogen had no interest in the penis wielding members of society then she would surely give Elfina a neutral opinion on the matter. Plus, she would not have competition for his affections from her blonde pretty friend.

That were unless he were secretly hiding a vagina under there...

No, no way. Each to their own but that was not him. He was all man...

Not that Elfina suspected that there was any competition. He only had sights for her so far that she could tell with his soft but penetrating gaze.

Not the only thing she wanted penetrating on seeing him! That fine, fine beast that she wanted to eat her up. He did not even glance at her companions that she sat with and instead he just stared her way as though she was a goddess sent from up above.

Which she wasn't.

Imogen was blonde and pure hearted. Most men zoned in on her first in their friendship group until they realised that she were actually a lesbian. Then they either admitted defeat or took their attention elsewhere.

Some turned nasty. They had seen it all on nights out. This was a relatively chilled night out for them with little attention aimed their way.

"Who?" Imogen turned round curiously to where her friend was gesturing to. Wondering with her facial expression what had taken her friends interest for the past few minutes. She frowned. Her blonde fringe lining her face as she stared.

At...nothing.

There was no one that side of the bar that Imogen could see of. Imogen looked back at her so sure friend with a firm frown still planted there. She swept her blonde hair from her face and frowned in her confusion.

"Who?"

"Him." Elfina turned her head to the side with a slight tilt and gestured with a hand towards the table where the man sat alone without even a glass of something strong to warm him up.

What were he drinking? Why was he there? But he was too bust staring at her in pure and utter awe to

"There`s no one there." Imogen said with no joke to her tone. She then giggled, probably thinking maybe she were the butt of Elfina`s jokes. Like usual.

"Why are you laughing?"

"Because you said there is someone there when that side of the bar is empty!" Imogen huffed and tried to explain.

"But there is." Elfina gestured again. "Look! Him."

Her friend looked round again. Each one adamant that they were right.

One saw someone, one saw no one.

"Elfina there is no one over there." Imogen whispered sharply and then turned to their mutual friends in a fuss. "Tell her, tell her there's no one over there." She pointed also with a lone finger.

She then snapped her fingers.

The others agreed firmly with Imogen with a nod, and all looked puzzled at their brunette adamant friend.

"Nope no one there,"

"What are you all looking at? Thin air!"

"Your pissing me off now!" Was her friend taking the piss? Elfina wondered.

Were they all? She stood up scuffing her chair back as the others grew concerned of her wellbeing in that moment. Maybe thinking that she had had quite a hectic day after her customers tragic death and it was why she were now seeing things from the strain of it all hitting her at once.

That the stress was getting to her.

That she were seeing things. Because she was surely? She was seeing him. But she did not want to see another. Only him.

Those blue eyes with swirls of black. That hair that she wanted caress. Those legs that she wanted to...

"Stay Elfina please. Its ok, you have had a crazy ass day. We all get them at times. We are here for you." Megan reassured her with a gentle touch as she hiccupped tipsily from drinking too fast.

She poured her confused friend a wine from her own personal bottle.

Privileged.

"But he`s over there!" Elfina hissed in annoyance and nodded to the hunk of her dreams who sat on his lonesome.

"Maybe Karl writing to you has made you, you know. A bit paranoid babe."

Elfina scowled at Megan. "Karl is not here, but someone else is! Him!"

Elfina turned her head back towards her dream man who was looking intently. He pulled her in to him much like a ufo would pull one in with its beam of light.

He was stood up now.

He beckoned her to come over with a finger. Oh, and his hands! She swooned again for special effect.

She felt butterflies reach her stomach as she swooned like a mere teen. She felt giddy, miraculous, all sorts of things in between them.

She meant to leave because no way in hell was, she letting that man leave alone. She had a pulse you know!

"He is leaving I have to go. Catch up soon guys." She quickly said to the three. She saw their puzzled reactions so to defuse the situation said, "Your probably right, the day has got to me. Talk soon. Toodle -loo." They looked concerned that she was staring into thin air and about to follow an invisible no one to who knows where.

Why couldn't they see him she asked herself? Was this a dream? If it were she wanted to stay asleep forever and to never wake up.

But no, the men in her dreams didn't wear long flowing coats like something out of the dark ages and wear tight leather trousers that showed off pert buns that she wanted to gently smack. They didn't also smell like whisky – her favourite drink, and a mix of white musk – her favourite scent in the whole wide world.

He started to leave for the door. Every so often looking back. Like a duck would as to make sure her ducklings were still there. Not leaving until he were for sure he were being followed.

By her.

And so, like maybe an idiot she followed him. A complete stranger? What were she thinking?

But apparently, she wasn't.

"Wait. Wait!" She called after him anxiously. She looked back one last time at her friends who were talking in a muddled hush and then looking at her like she had two heads or possibly three or four.

She staggered off from the bar taking her bottle as she went for, she needed it right then. Maybe regretting the last drink that she had, had before she scooted after him.

At last, she reached the cool of the outside and felt the breeze hit her blushed face.

The guy was exactly where she wanted him to be.

"Not here." He said as he was waiting for her by the exit then seemed antsy.

"Then where?"

"Follow me." The guy crooned to her and nodded towards further down the street out of the ears of others.

His voice were silky, smooth, but still so darned manly that it made her throb. She would have paid anything to hear his voice again so soon. Should she follow a random man, in the now dark of the city so late at night? And one that no one but her could, see?

Dicey...

No, not really. Stranger danger and all as her awful mother had taught her, although her uncaring mother were actually the one, she had needed saving from. But he could be an axe murderer, a serial killer.

A beast.

Mmm... maybe a sexy beast, she blushed as she took him in from head to toe.

But something was different here and she could sense it without yet knowing what it were. She felt that he had the answers that she seeked so desperately.

She nodded politely with a lowering of the head and followed him nervously. She felt that she already would go after him even if he had not requested it of her.

After a time of walking down one street then two, she stopped behind him as he stopped suddenly with a grinding halt. Nearly running right into the back of him as he gave no warning of it.

The mystery man dressed like something from years ago but who rocked the look with ease said, "Here, here will do although we really need somewhere private for this with what I have to say to you."

Was she imagining it or had he a hint of red appeared in his blue, stony gaze? But even then, she was still not scared one bit, but she did not quite know why.

"Why, why did you want me to follow you?" She asked with a stutter for he was intimidating. As if power circled around him.

He looked at her with interest and then spoke with his tuneful voice that made her pussy want to sing, "My, your voice is so fucking beautiful Elfina. It is almost as beautiful as you yourself are. I could listen to you speak all day to me and not tire of it in any way. But I wanted you to follow me for one reason, and one reason only. Because if we had talked there back at that questionable bar that you were in then everyone would have questioned your sanity."

He held her gaze, he made her quake, she wanted to shake.

Or cum from the fear and arousal that were taking over.

"My sanity?" She squeaked.

"Your sanity, my lady." His eyes bore through hers.

Right into her very soul. She did not now know where he started, and she finished as he had stepped that close to her with silent booted steps that they were now eye to eye. Mouth to mouth. But he were taller then she, so he had to lower his head to watch her.

To be her equal. But could she ever be an equal to a male this this. She was considered pretty she knew this. But his looks were-unquestionable....

"Fuck my sanity!" She scoffed that unfazed and threw her hands out to make her point. He laughed warmly as she spoke which made a cosy feeling run through her.

What were that? Contentment perhaps. Or the nearest that she could actually get to it.

To her slight surprise he reached out a large hand and cupped her cheek lightly with it and gazed adoringly at her like she were his everything. She wondered what his long fingers could do to her when they were playing her like a fiddle as he stroked her blushed cheek in caress.

She were stumped for words; he would have to be the one to next talk.

He whispered. "Elfina. My Elfina." He almost groaned it in pleasure. She wondered what he would sound like groaning her name as he came?

How did he know her name she thought coming out oof her aroused daze? But still she did not feel in any way threatened by him or at ease like she had done with her infamous letter writer.

She needed answers and so brattily stomped a foot onto the paved ground, "I am not your Elfina! You can't take claim to someone that you don't know... man. But... how did you know my name anyway strange foreign man from who knows where? Who are you even? Did he send you? Am I...am I mad for seeing you when others cannot get a glimpse

Iden leapt without thinking into an ill prepared speech, "No, no you are not mad. You might be your own person, your own soul, your own keeper. But when I have been waiting hundreds if not thousands of years for you to take your place by my side, then am I not entitled to call you my own one?" Iden groaned then continued on.

"Mad, we are all mad my darlin, and I may be the maddest of them all as such for that is why I make the best leader. But I would be mad, if it meant keeping you with me for all of eternity if madness is what it takes to keep you there."

"Ok..." She felt overwhelmed but a pull still to the guy, but backed away at his sheer intensity and what it could so mean. It was almost if he was an old soul trapped in a young ones body by the way that he spoke.

Mysterious or what!

He took a bold step forward. His feet were huge she noticed! Well huge feet must mean huge something else...she guessed.

Iden uttered adoringly, "If you take a step back, I will take a step forward and then we will be here all evening my now dearest one. There is much to be said... Elfina." He breathed this almost huskily, "Heck even your name is unworldly to me. It is divine, quite like you are."

"My aunt chose it as my parents could not be bothered to name me, they were that up and down." She snapped this and then gasped. Why had she told a virtual stranger that piece of info about her upbringing?

She did not know why.

But did it matter? No, not really, it did not. Not now that the words had been spoken out loud and that there was no taking them back to be put back in her mouth.

What he said next, she could not in a million years have expected. It made her chest ache and her stomach turn over at the unexpectedness of it.

He studied her for a moment with a raised groomed brow. "Did she also name your sister. Little Ruby?" In a fierce growl.

She gasped again at hearing her sisters name by a stranger, but it were harder, the air almost left her plump chest with it and her head spun in a simple daze.

She grabbed on to a nearby wall for support. He came closer as though he himself were her support.

"Ruby?" Her chest felt cold. She felt panic. Just breathe Elfina, breathe dammit! In, out, in, out. It's not hard she ordered herself as she felt panic!

"Ruby." He repeated and nodded gently with softened eyes. There was worry behind his beautiful eyes though. He was troubled by something. But now were not the time as he had mentioned her dear sister again.

Now a whole can of worms had been opened up that would be impossible to stuff back into the god damned can because they would only spill out.

Ruby... She raged at him, "My sister is dead sir! Mister, whoever you bloody well are. How do you know of her? What is she to you or what were she before?"

He traced her arm with a lone, thick finger that caused a cool chill to go down her spine, "She is anything but dead Elfina."

His eyes went completely red the colour of her own blood, and she shuddered as he looked at her slender neck with strange interest like he wanted to take out a chunk of her, to bite it.

To saviour it.

He sniffed her openly, inhaled her, much like a dog would do to another dogs bottom that they were getting to know. Awkward.

"Don't sniff me!" She moved back and away from his weird sniffing of her person.

She should go, leave there she decided uneasily. Leave him. Go home to the safety of her own home and shut the door and bolt it tightly so else no one could get in to it. Her sweet own haven. But yet even though his blue kinda black eyes had gone a shade of red, she was not scared of him or what he might do to her.

Only impatient to know.

Curious yeah, bewildered even more so.

Fascinated but still not scared by any means.

"She is alive then?" Her painted lips, her made up face oh so full of hope at this he could see, but she knew hand on heart that her beloved sister truly wasn't in the land of the living... She would have reached out to her by now if she were. If she could. She would have been the first one to step in for her when Karl had reached his peak.

And came back again. Again, and again. Since her attack, there had been only nothing from her...The only explanation was that she couldn't.

He paused as though thinking how to reply and then shook his head sadly. It were like he felt her pain for his own and then held it there with respect for her.

Iden sighed, "Also no. Do you have somewhere that we can talk freely away from here? I promise not to sniff you again. Unless you want me to that is?" He smiled and stuck out a rather unexpected thick tongue that made her twitch at the thought of what it could do in one`s panties.

That it could possibly bring her to her knees and keep her there.

She shook her wild thoughts away from her perverse thoughts and smiled at the thought of spending more time with this marvellous, mysterious man. Never having being attracted to a man like this before in quite this way. This intensity.

Nor she suspected she ever would...

She smiled eagerly, her caution non-existent, "I would like that. You can come back to mine. I think...." She was in two minds.

"Oi, oi!" He jested and winked at her offer with no hidden meaning.

"Not for that." She scolded him with a waggle of the finger.

"No, I was joking with you love. For a chat. That would be for the best. Not here. Not now."

"Your name. I can`t invite someone in if I do not know there name." Elfina said confidently as she remembered that she had not asked him for it. And he had not offered it either, but she wanted to know of it.

"Iden. Fortheart."

"Iden." She copied the sound. Sounding his name out slowly and rolling it over her tongue to get used to saying. "That is an unusual name." For it were so.

"Well, I am an unusual person." He pouted teasingly.

"That you are. You can come in to talk but no sex involved. At all. And when I tell you to leave buddy. You leave." She spoke sharply and pointed in what she hoped was a menacing way.

Not realising she were talking to a very old, very real- vampire.

If he wanted to, he could hurt someone, anyone.

But not her.

He felt aroused at her blazing dominance and his cheeks flushed in his own rude thoughts much like her.

"I can do that." He grinned. "As tempting as it would be to take you in my arms and make sweet love until you cannot walk... I stand by what you say."

She looked at his smiling mouth. His lips were strangely thin, thinner then hers, but she still could reach out and kiss him. Hold his lips to hers and eat him alive with her tongue!

Say what! She did not even know the guy. She noted how pale his skin were. As though he did not get much sun. Or he lived in a cold country. It were even paler then her own skin which was fair as can be. She had always been envious of her friend Megan with her tanned skin or Lovella with her warm cocoa own one.

She herself resembled the bride of a vampire almost if such myths existed!

She bossed him again, he seemed to like it strangely, she could tell he did. "And do something with the eyes. It`s freaky. Why are they changing colour?"

"The eyes they have a mind of their own love. I will try to turn them back to blue with a hint of black, but I make no promises that I can achieve that in any way. I have been around for many, many years, even before you but still my eyes they change when they so choose to do so."

Ok then...

Years? He looked if she squinted to be in his twenties, maybe early thirties if that. This was becoming more like a fairy tale, a fantasy, an imagination as each second passed them on while the moon shone bright in the night sky.

They had at last after what had seemed like endless walking reached the sanctuary of her shop, with of course her flat high above it. Her home.

She sighed as she had to decide now where the next step lay. To let him in or to keep on walking past as though she did not live there at all?

For he might look like a night, but he could be a demon in disguise.

He looked up at the sign with a tilted head with interest.

'Elfina`s.'

"This is ...your own place? Wow I am impressed I must say." He looked at the sigh again.

She blushed a shade of crimson that brought the colour out on her pale skin.

"Yes, yes, it is Iden. Now come. You have the answers and I have the questions." He did not answer but made to go inside as she turned her head and fumbled with the lock to get in. Her phone was dinging with what he guessed where from messages or calls from her concerned friends.

"Pardon love?" A nearby blonde, short middle-aged stumpy man said on passing them. Who stunk of alcohol and had a dubious look about him. She gasped as she realised shakily that it was only her that could likely see this mysterious, tall, handsome male behind her

Had she lost the plot? She still didn't think so but maybe. Maybe. It was all too real. From his looks, his scent, the awe dropping humungous pull between them. There was no imagining that.

"Nothing I was just talking to myself sir." She tried to explain nicely although she didn't want to, for her silent creep alarm was dining a loud tune that would not stop. She shuddered and felt a moment of panic as the drunk staggered closer. Closer. Closer.... She could smell the scent of alcohol as if it was, she that had consumed it.

"Want me to help you with the door?" The blonde, stubby man leered and then looked around she guessed, to make sure that they would not be disturbed. That they were alone. Not realising that there were an invisible, possibly thousand-year-old vampire staring him out from behind with pure and utter hatred.

Who could eat him, spit him out and feel no remorse or shame to doing it. Who would enjoy it.

Before she could answer, before she could speak there was a loud growl solely from her hidden hero which proved his existence unless she were hearing things also. He looked so angry, so fierce.

So, fucking handsome.

His face though began resembling a monster like straight out of a film. Claws stretched out of his hands instead of his neat nails. Fangs left his sharp mouth. Sprang out as if to bite.

Fuck he were beautiful.

All she could do were stare in awe and wonder at the invisible to all others - monster. She could stare all day it seemed. What was wrong with her, was she a monster fucker or something?

No, no she were not. Yet. But she could be if that was what he were!

"Mine!" He growled out to the stranger in strained despair. But not in a way like that someone had taken his last jelly tot from his grasp. In a way like that someone had taken the most important thing from him in his life, and he would pound them into concrete to avenge them.

Break their skull into two and use it as a set of ashtrays.

His fated mate at risk from a lousy drunk.

Though she were not yet aware of this.

The drunk man looked round for who was there joining him, sensing no one but feeling something, hearing something, and the younger woman that he had latched his creepy drunken gaze on. Already in a state of confusion by smelling a man to the side but then not confused enough to scare poor Elfina.

For sadly she had dealt with far worse from Karl.

He had shown her what true evil could be. This drunk there was an amateur.

The man on hearing footsteps in a panic grabbed her arm surprisingly with stubby yet clammy fingers, and she shook it free from him, "What, what were that?" He trembled and shook at the next spectacular growl from someone, something that he could not place.

Because the threat were invisible to him.

He had heard rumours as he were of the older generation of beasts that attacked in the night but that no one could see. Or maybe they were merely just drunks like him? No, he sensed that were not true.

"If only you could see." She said to the whino with a sure glint in her eye at the drunks puzzlement. For she were now no longer alone in her peril and if she could not get this pest to leave her then she would bet her life savings (not much) that Iden would do it.

She did not know him, but she knew without a doubt, from his invisible hold, the way he looked at her, watched her, seemed to want her for his own, said that she were the one he had been waiting for whatever that meant to them?

That he would protect her until the end of time.

She watched in horror that was not expected as the door lock stuck as the stranger started to take out a long, thin but obviously sharp knife from his pocket, causing fear for Elfina. She shook and sweated at the sight of it. Her chest felt tight, and she almost wheezed in her panic.

Not knowing what to do there. Should she stand still as still could be? See what the man did before she reacted to it, before she chose what to do? Scream, shout or fight back in any way possible? For there were no way on hells earth that she would be taken out, evilly used, like her poor lovely sister had assumed to of been.

She would not let him if she could. For her sake and for her sister. She needed questions to where her sister were.

And also, there were now fear for Iden. If his mate got hurt, then he would shove that knife so far up the man's arse that it would come out his mouth the other end.

Woah!

The man still held it unsurely as if unsure whether to take it out of his pocket and do something with it as he latched onto it.

The suspense was currently killing Iden. Either way, the man he knew would not be leaving alive for daring to touch what was his and his alone. He was a man of honour as taught by his own mother many hundreds of years ago, that woman should be loved, worshiped and cherished and adored with every fibre of their being.

Iden then snarled, his huge, sharp fangs giving him a slight lisp, He spoke angrily, "Put the knife away you drunkard or else I will gut you with it and disembowel you. Leave, and never darken her door again or any other innocent females besides!" He spoke like he were from another time.

Which he were of course.

The drunk man was out of there in an instant at the threat. Running on worn boots, his arms flapping in the light wind. His knife fell to a clang on the floor and Iden swooped into recover it.

The retreating guy possibly shat his pants.

"Thank you." She said to the red eyed hottie with sincerity.

Iden did not react, not yet, but he stopped for a moment as in a trance like state. Like he had headphones in and was listening to something of importance. Then he shook his head to the side as though he were coming out of it.

Free from his engulfed daze.

He ordered like a naughty school teacher in his deep commanding voice, "Get in the shop Elfina. I have to go it is highly important that I do so. I must. But I will be back, I promise you that Elfina." He tried to smile but it resembled a lion stalking its prey as though he had to go but wanted to stay and devour her.

She looked sad at this, "Do... you have to? I wanted to talk about Ruby. I wanted to talk about this..." She gestured to them both.

"I really must. I am sorry. If I don't then it might be the last of me,"

"I understand."

"Do you?" He said.

"Yes, I think so...." Before she could speak further, he grabbed her softly and pushed his lips firmly to hers. Their lips met in pure, needy hunger and their tongues entwined.

It was so fast that by the time she had worked out that he was kissing her he had pulled away with a lingering gaze that made her melt and throb.

Knowing that when he had grabbed her that the hard thing sticking into her wasn't one of his swords from before. But something else that she so desperately wanted to see, to touch, to feel, lick...

She then watched him back up from her and then to her absolute wonder, and to her sudden shock he sprouted out the most hugest, wonderous black wings from his toned back as though it were an everyday occurrence for him.

Although it must be. For they were real and all the more- firmly attached to him.

Wow....What she would give to touch them. Would they feel soft as feathers? Would he fuck her while his wings stood out and proud?

"Don`t be..." She whispered astounded by this man from nowhere.

He took off from the ground in an instant as though he simply weighed nothing. She imagined being in his large, toned arms, being carried through the night sky by him and circling the moon round and round as the stars lit the sky.

Would that ever happen one day?

She flushed.

She felt sorry to see him go. And then a sad pang in her chest as he left as though they were now somehow connected to each other with an invisible thread that only they could feel.

She as he glided away looked round carefully for the creepy ass, drunk man to ensure that he was not hanging around like a bad smell for a chance to pounce yet again, but he was nowhere to be seen thankfully for her.

And for him.

For you should be able to walk home without random people trying to do you harm, trying to steal things, doing things that to you they should not do.

She took a deep and large thankful breath as she entered the safety of her shop filled with the alarms and cameras that gave her some protection or so she hoped. Maybe she should get one for the entrance hall she thought on a whim?

As she was closing the door to, blocking the outside life out from her own bubble she heard a loud masculine scream that sounded just like - the drunk man from off outside.

Her brows hit the ceiling.

No surely not she thought in puzzlement? Where had Iden gone to in a hurry? And wings? Like the stuff from mere fantasies, he was so magnificent that she could cry just by looking at him.

She shut the door to, locked up in a fleeting hurry and then tiredly plodded up the flight of stairs on padded feet whilst trying not to trip up the loose stair carpet that had caught her unawares before.

She went off and into her living room after checking all of the rooms to make sure that she was truly alone in there, poured herself a large wine from her plentiful well stocked supply that she had, for she needed it and greeted the small, fluffy dog who was so happy to see her that his tail was going a clapper and he was drooling from where his tongue stuck out, out at the corner of his mouth.

He came bounding over with all sorts of remarkable barks to tell of.

After letting him go out begrudgingly because she had to unlock all the doors to and to then lock up tightly again, she got up the CCTV footage rapidly on her phone on her app from her ring doorbell, on the shop.

Clicking through the settings until she zoned in on the recent footage. Not thinking to look at the footage of when the customer passed as of yet, and she heard the eerie yet remarkable singing.

Instead concentrating on the now. Eagerly hoping to catch another glimpse of – him. With her own eyes.

Clutching the buzz inducing wine in trembling, clammy fingers, she then watched with eager eyes curiously as the recent conversations on the screen play out with a nervous and serious expression to her oval face.

Pause then rewind. What the heck? It looked to be like at first glance that she were simply standing around talking to herself on the screen, but she then heard a mumbling when Iden were talking although one could not make out the words in any shape or form or otherwise. It was as an idea came to her what could be going on that maybe the frequency could not be picked up by most human ears and of recent tech.

She then on the screen saw the weird staggering man appear from out of the fog, then she heard it – the eerie wolf like growl. She rewound it and fast. Her fingers tapping to find the right place at the right time.

There!

She heard it again. An animalistic growl that on hearing it again was neither beast like nor human like either.

Oh, thank god, she thought! She were not going crazy after all like she had had an inkling that she were. She knew that her friends must do also. She hoped that he would be back she thought as she got ready for bed in her favourite silky pyjamas after brushing her teeth and tying her hair up.

The ones that made her feel oh so fine although she did alas not have anyone to show them off to. Would Iden like them? She wondered what pyjamas he wore. He to her looked like maybe a naked bed wearer. Or was that just wishful thinking?

She through a curious gaze, watched the last of the footage that had occurred just before she entered her shop for the night. She waited patiently stood still with anticipation for some action doubting that there would be any, but then as her heart beat quickened, she heard what sounded like a man yelp and then an ear-piercing scream.

It was the drunk man.

There was no question of that. It could be no one else besides him. A feeling of dread hit her for a moment, only merely a moment and she briefly looked out of the window but could not really see a thing as fog was thickening outside. But also, she cruelly smiled inside and felt some kind of strange buzzing satisfaction that, that man had felt something, felt terror when she had seen his knife, just like she had done....

Fear. Terror. And all alone. He would not have a guardian in black wings to protect him.

Merely one to destroy him...

The door made her jump as it banged too, and so she hot footed it down there after grabbing a long coat. Iden! Could it be he? Back for her. She felt sick with nerves and more than a little bit tipsy as the wine kicked in some more. She got to the front door with great speed and stupidly forgot to check the keyhole to see who it were or to leave the chain on in her upmost excitement.

She opened it wide and proud.

"Iden?"

"Who the fucks Iden..." A familiar voice said in a snarl.

"Karl!" She gasped in pure horror. Feeling that she could have kicked herself for not being more careful when answering the door to the fearsome knock that had awaited her.

"Hello Elfina." Dark brown and bushy brows and creepy eyes gazed at her. He smiled with a lopsided grin that showed off his crooked teeth.

Iden`s were nicer. Much nicer.

In an ill-fitting suit(she highly doubted that Iden would be seen dead in that either) and dark blonde scruffy hair, a messy beard with a hint of moustache growing in. He did not look good for his thirties.

Ok, he looked like shit.

But it was his personality that had always bothered her, nothing else. Looks didn't matter it was attraction, and she had neither to him. He talked over her all the time, he thought that she was being stubborn when she weren't. When really, she was just not interested in him or being with him.

Elfina did not play games with Karl. She had not led him on in any way, but he had refused to leave her alone once she did not want to see him anymore.

In her mind that made him as bad as the men that had hurt her sister.

But at least they were dead. Karl was still alive and kicking and still causing trouble for her.

Maybe others. Was there others? Still not taking no for an answer! She guessed not.

She gasped in pure undiluted horror, ice coldness swivelled around her on seeing his face again. Her heart pounded in her chest and her pearly teeth chattered with the cool air that nipped. She felt panicky like she had been here before.

But she had.

This man there, there was no getting away from. He did not sadly understand the word no. To him no meant maybe which was not the right way. No was no. It should mean it!

Her dog barked behind her as he tried to step in to her sanctuary.

"Get off!" She yelled as he touched her arm with a firm grip and one heck of a snarl and tried to pull her towards him.

When Iden had touched her, it felt like heaven. The touch of Karl only meant hell...

"So where are we living now then?" He said to her as he pushed past her and tore up the stairs in scuffed boots...

Luckily at the bottom of the door was a pair of trainers as she were in bare feet and her bag. She grabbed the shoes and put them hastily on.

She picked her dog up and ran for her life. Not caring where she went, she just wanted out of there. The dog yipped in agreement.

He hated Karl.

CHAPTER SIX

I DEN
  Iden could not believe the vision that met him in the semi crowded bar on first swivelling gently down to earth. He had waited around for hours bored on feeling a pull to the place since arrival. It must be where she were.

His one.

Surely?

He had sat there and had to move as he was nearly sat on. He watched with interest a fight over a woman. A disagreement over money.

Later on, as he grew weary a group of woman in their late twenties possibly older came cluttering into the bar noisily drawing the surrounding single males gazes like hawks, the usual woman that vacated bars like this one - loud, silly and chattering on about work, make -up and what not.

A dark-skinned curvy woman lifted a hand to summon the busy barman who looked like he would rather amputate his own legs with a hack saw then be there at his current place of work.

A tall blonde built like a model who were slim but slightly curved accompanied her.

A smaller but thin brunette hiding a bottle of whisky in her bag-heck Ashley would suit someone like her, he chuckled quietly so that no one could hear!

After all, laughing loudly with a more then mad chuckle when no one could see you, was probably what had led to all the ghost investigations that had taken place over the human world.

And then there were simply – her. It must be.

Wow.

She did not notice him so at first for a while even though they should have been drawn together like simple magnets. He stood there nervously twitching his fingers together, flexing his arms. Trying to stay in one position nervously and not grab her and run!

And instead, so unsure of what to do, what to say or how to act, because heck – no one on earth except earth living vamps could even see him in this bar or elsewhere besides that. Even a vampires mate on earth would not be able to see him except for his own destined one.

Her. His Elfina.

He could not drink either for they would only see a floating whisky glass at an empty table. And all the screams would put him off his drink that he wanted to savour! Plus, he could hardly recommend his own clan to stay away from human activities, to remain on the down low then to go off gallivanting into a bar himself to get merry and slightly wasted!

Now, now it did not bother him the fact that no one could see him there. He could be childish and pull stupid faces at unsuspecting customers, pee down an alley with his large cock and his pert bum out and not fear being disturbed or watched by those in long anoraks with a hand on their own one.

He could stand right near someone without looking like a creep and they could only feel him breathe, not see him. And to Knick their greasy chips and battered sausage when they turned their back and when there was no one else in view.

Make them think that they were going mad.

It humoured him.

At the start after his transfusion into - well this, what he were now – the living dead, it had been so bloody awful and lonely for him, and it made him feel even more down then before he died.

Like being a ghost. Except people saw ghosts. He, they did not. Had not. Could not.

Didn't they?

"Why can't you see me?" He had cried to himself the first time after his death that he had gone down to earth not long afterwards. But it had felt like no one had seen him before he had died. That was in part what had caused him to revert to should we say – drastic and permanent measures.

After his brother had changed him into an immortal, blood sucking being against his will, he had visited his old run down home out of missing and curiosity.

On arriving his parents and sister were there as always with stony, yet teary faces eating met and veg and some potatoes – or trying to anyway.

He had stood and watched from the front of the shabby place; his handsome face pressed against the entrance of it as they cried openly for him and his forever death. Even his big beloved dad was in bits at the table.

Or they cried for the lack of him.

For he were the missing, the missing he would remain, but his body remained forever with him for all time, and it would for all of eternity. He would not get sick; he would not die or remain injured for too long. He would just be him until the very end.

Iden the vampire.

They would never find him or his corpse for there was not one. And there would be no tear-streaked burial with all wearing black. Except Rennie, she would wear some form of pink if she could get away with it. For pink would suit her. It was bright like she had been. Although she were a long time dead now to his utter sadness.

He could smell their sweet blood from there where he stood lingering out in the shadows. He was a newbie vamp, so it smelt to him like the finest thing that he had ever smelt in his short life. He drooled as the scent hit the back of his throat that it made him gulp.

His eyes grew red. Then back again as he urged himself not to go in there and cause their death.

Yes, drooled like a madman at his own bloody family! How sick did that make him? Not at the food that was one of his favourite meals there on the table, but the food that ran through their veins.

The food that could not be eaten but drunk.

Human tantalising blood.

"I`m not dead mum!" He had felt like screaming at her loudly in his ever winding – ever growing so tremendous pain as he had collapsed onto his knees on the dirty ground. His cloak that he liked to wear flapping around him as he fell onto the dirt.

He wanted to shake his mother so fucking much like a doll, to then pull her so darn tight to him and to never let go as she were the one to always comfort her wayward son when he had needed it.

To talk and let her listen like they used to do on various occasions when it was just them- mother and son. But he sadly could not let on that he were even there to them. For else if he did with a feeling of unease in his stomach, he knew that he would not be back.

He would outgrow them all. He could not watch them die.

Nor could he find it in himself to turn them into a monster like him. And he knew Rhys wouldn't either.

He had only turned him to punish him. That is what Iden guessed.

He could not go in there to his old home in the country. He would scare them, possibly bleed them dry with the hunger that he felt so deep to the bones that it cursed him inside.

So invisible- he should remain.

But then with a flutter of miraculous wings, his elder brother, his over eager sire, his one and only saviour but also the bringing of this god damn curse that ran through him had then flown down to him there on the ground.

Stood there by his side as he got up off the ground, like the brothers that they truly were. Rhys put a large brotherly hand on his shoulder to still him, to feel his discomfort with his own, and he were the taller one of the two.

The strongest. But only just.

Showing a rare bit of emotion for his brothers temporarily pain and permanent losing of his humanity. Some of it that he had caused himself for sure, but also some of his brothers own making.

The elder one with his long brown hair and firm muscles, shook his head and side eyed Iden with a slight glare.

"Let them go Iden." His brows firmly in line like he were angry with him but yet- not. He had always been there to guide his younger brother, to shield him, to protect him although he normally had his own back.

Even though they did not see eye to eye and his brother did not trust him.

They were blood brothers.

And blood brothers they would remain.

"I cannot." Iden sighed in deflated reply. It had hurt to try.

"That must be the way. I had to let them go too you know. But I saw the chance to have you with me for all time when I received the call that day. I knew it were you."

"Pah! We thought you were dead Rhys, and now they are going through it all over again with another child. It is not fair!" It was not right in Iden's opinion to make them endlessly suffer that way. To have lost two out of three kids was more than one could so bare.

"It was either that or they would have found your body battered and broken at the bottom of a cliff somewhere my smaller brother. What version of events would be easier for them to take in do you think? A crumpled suicide victim or a missing one?" His eyes narrowed into his smaller brothers own ones.

"I thank you for that brother. I do now. But you did not give me the choice to be as I wanted and when I said I needed to think but it was unlikely not as I did not deserve to live, you said there were no time to wait and decide. So now I am here, and they are there. Invisible to them and I cannot tell them that I am still somewhere out there in this whole bloody world. Their sons are invisible to them! It is almost laughable, if it wasn't so darn sad."

"They know that you are gone they must feel it in their hearts. They found your stuff and some clothes at the cliffs where you were last seen. Your pitiful good bye scrawled on a tablet perhaps. You should have died fighting like me, fighting like a real man." His brother hissed, "But yet you took the easy way out or tried to anyway. There is no easy way-out brother. With that you are here. Here with me. In our own hidden realm with our own hidden clans. Clans they cannot be a part of not ever. So, you can either let them go and be at peace right now or you can go in there, show yourself, well your voice anyway and send our parents to an early grave once you devour them. For either way you will outlive them all. Even our poor sister Reenie." Rhys spat.

And with that as the rain fell down, Rhys flew away off into the distance with his own back wings. Probably off to rip through the neck of a harboured criminal or to even charm one of the newer vamps with his temptingly seductive ways.

And not long after that the wedge between them truly began.

CHAPTER SEVEN

IDEN

Iden raced back to the vampire realm as fast as he could possibly do so with his bare wings fluttering behind him. Faster than a bird, faster than a thrown boomerang, he got home in the nick of time.

He had only stopped on the way so as to drain the alcoholic man half dry who had dared to shake his beloved, fated mate up with a sharp pointed weapon.

For being bled out, bled full dry, would be no lesson at all to the daring guy. Now the sozzled stinking man would simply look like a drunk loon when he talked to others about what he had seen and hopefully - well Iden hoped, that he had given him enough of a scare to not proposition woman like that ever again.

He hoped that his bite had pained him.

Because if he did do what he did again then he would be spending the rest of his time somewhere rather hot and low down...

Iden then unfortunately had, had an urgent matter to attend to – hence the trance like state that Elfina had witnessed him getting into briefly.

"Clan meeting now. All available members who are not soul collecting must come and no other excuses are permitted!" He had snapped at Ashley who were the first member that he had bumped into on arriving back home.

Appearing that he had just been to his as he turned around. Great.

Ashley frowned deeply and stared with brown eyes and bumbled out. "What`s wrong?" He obviously knew that it must be an urgent matter for Iden to call an unexpected clan meeting out of the blue and in such a hurry to.

There had been no answer only an annoyed scowl.

"Ok give me an hour. You chose a bad time. It is late."

"We have all the time in the world to sleep Ash."

"That we do. Ok as I said give me an hour. If they are all snarly with tiredness at this said meeting then it is on you."

"No. Quicker! Fuck the tiredness."

"For fucks sake! I will try."

Ashley had even put his expensive, top of the range whisky bottle clutched in his grip down and not even taken it and had then sped off in a hurry to summon all others possible. For keeping the boss waiting he knew would not do.

While Ashley sped off, Iden turned round and noticed his door to his huge open had swung open.

"Darn you, Ashley!" Iden scowled crossly on seeing it and knowing what it meant.

That matter must be addressed also then. His complete and utter lack of privacy with his clan. He had just restocked the fridge, and all so there would be hell to pay if his new blood supply were missing as well as his alcohol going!

He would rip his friend a new one before he let him take his blood!

He went into his home to inspect for damages and missing items. Luckily, he found that his friend had more sense than he thought as his fridge remained seemingly full. He looked through it, past the sparce food and pulled out a vial of blood. His mouth watered and his stomach growled like he had not eaten in weeks.

He greedily drunk the red nectar that awaited him. Not wanting to spill a drop because that would not do. He needed to keep a clear head and with no blood in his system apart from the drunk man's intoxicating one during the meeting and he would have likely gone nuclear!

Fuck it he wanted more he surprisingly realised on finishing it! Which was surprising as he had had half of the drunk man's delicious goods too! Normally they did not need to feed so often but he was stressed among other things what with Elfina and her sister...

He pulled out another vial and held it in his cool grasp firmly and then grabbed another, and then when he were truly on the last vial-

"Iden what are you doing?!" A stunned voice rang out.

He turned his head shadily around with blood dripping down his mouth rather like he were a newbie vamp and not a senior one with control, a clan leading, nearly thousand-year-old vampire. With his fangs sharply out and too wound up to put them back into his mouth.

His glazed eyes were crimson red, and he were now in what was known as a blood daze. Vampires usually only hit that specific point when they were really totally blood deprived, but in rare instances they could also when they had been rationing somewhat – and their emotions could set them off.

Like now. His were all over the place.

Iden pined for his mate.

Badly. He wanted her so fucking badly that the distance apart, the realms that kept them, physically hurt him in every way possible and if he even needed to breathe, which he didn't it would hurt him to do so with each breath he took. How would it hurt a weaker immortal to be apart from his dull likely mate Susan, like- say Geoffrey?

He regretted the way that he had spoken to the annoying buffoon now. If he had known what it felt like to be away from your own destiny, away from your own heart, he would have egged him on.

He would have not caused the needless drama that he had caused before the inspiration party, Geoffrey's send off.

But now the way that he were, downing the blood like it were merely juice – he would be a danger to her and all that she ever cared about!

"I`m... just having a quick drink." He explained through his blood-filled haze.

"It seems that way. The meeting has been called. Do you mind telling me why you are drinking all the blood vials that I know u painfully got hold of to fill that fridge? Even I tempted as I were knew not to take any... What is troubling you?" Ashley asked.

"I found her Ash."

"Found who?" His friends brown eyes honed in on his dark blue ones with deep interest. He was evidently not aware what had happened that day. That the meeting of Iden's mate would soon likely have a knock-on effect for them all.

That Ruby and her suspected mate finding could bring peace to the whole entire realm. Because surely even his own brother who was at rock bottom in the depths of despair in the darkness, would settle down once he had found what it were he were looking for?

His dark mate.

"My mate, my friend. And Ruby led the way to her door. My brother took her. He took little Ruby."

"Woah. Woah, woah. One thing at a time. Say what?"

Iden threw his empty vial across the room with a victorious smash. Not meaning to hit his second he was just trying to let off some steam. Walking over to his friend he repeated everything. "Ruby saw her sister Elfina. For some reason or another she realised that her sister is... my fated mate." He said.

"What!"

Iden continued on, ignoring his friends exasperation.

"It is true. I have seen her for myself. And she takes my breath away. For she is simply...divine." He sighed like an obsessed boy teen holding a signed movie poster of his idol. "Rhys came for an unfortunate visit here and he somehow thought that he smelt his mate on Ruby and stupidly thought she herself was his own mate, and so he took her after knocking me out with some weird creation of his. If he was not my own flesh and blood, I swear down I would kill him myself and show him no mercy!" He growled and grunted.

His friend stiffened and he grew wide eyed.

"Jeez poor Ruby! Hmm. Say I wonder if she can find my own fated one? Congratulations Iden. I am so pleased for you. You have been waiting a long time, it is well deserved."

For it were.

They were that close that each one finding their fated mate was as glorious as if they had found their own.

Iden noticed the lack of caring about poor Ruby from Ashley. They hadn't bonded at all in any way, but she had instead veered more towards the friendship of Barren where they could be childlike and play together games and watch movies.

Barren did not judge her.

"And of Ruby?" Iden dared to ask.

"Well, I mean of course I am worried. But she can handle herself as you have seen her do Iden."

"If you had seen the state she were in when I collected her then you would not even utter that, Ash."

"I am sorry but none of us are in the know as it her business and hers alone and I don't wish to pry into what led her to this realm that day."

"Or you don't care enough?" Iden hissed, his fangs protruded in anguish.

Ashley appeared stricken. "It is not that. She will be fine. Especially if he thinks she is his cos even your brother would treasure the one he thought was his."

"He slapped her."

"Oh." Ashley gave up with the whole argument. "I`m guessing once he has settled down then we can sort something out between ourselves. But today is a day of celebration. Congratulations again."

"Thank you, my friend. There will be enough time for congratulations later once I have dealt with the... more important things that are going on." Too many things to mention as of yet.

Sometimes being clan leader was like being a juggler but whereas the balls were slippery, oh yeah, then on fire too. And there were too many of them. That was what Iden`s life were like in that moment.

"Such as?" Ashley said curiously running a dark hand through his also dark curled hair. He was sweating very slightly from endlessly running around most of the realm like a madman trying to get as many vamps as possible to come to a late ass meeting that no one wanted to.

But they all must if they could, all in Iden`s clan anyway. If the matter continued, then he would have to reach out much further.

"Someone has not been doing their soul collecting."

Ashley gasped in horror at this notion.

For surely no one would dream of actually not turning up to collect the dead for their trip to the beyond. Well maybe in a few rare circumstances such as when Ruby and Iden had murdered the four attackers in cold blood and a frantic frenzy of biting and sucking, arm and leg ripping. But he had not long after gotten someone else to take the violent souls off out and on their way.

To not collect them.... No one did that. Not even stuck-up vamps like Justina did that to his knowledge. Heck even Rhys without his heart to name of did what he had to!

It was who they were. Soul collecting vampires!

"And I'm about going to find out who...."

L ater that eve Iden was at the clan headquarters. It had always reminded him of Wembley stadium in the way that it appeared and the whole shape of it. He had never been in Wembley as it was after his time of course for he was as old as shit, but he had eyes and ears and that was what it reminded him of.

Plus, he watched telly.

If the realm did not have telly's he would go mad from boredom. A vampire needed hobbies after all!

It needed to be a large venue what with all the clan members that he had who needed to fit in.

He and Ashley walked firmly through the magnificent entrance and proceeded towards the main hall of the place for there were several of them located there. They entered it and Iden were pleased to note that someone had organised the drinks and nibbles for the talk in which he hoped it wouldn't be long at all.

It looked to be a good turn out in the short amount of time that it had taken Ash to round everybody up.

Wine glasses and pitchers full of blood or blood 2.0 as they nicknamed it - the fake stuff. That was for the few veggies or vegans that they had who refused to down something directly from a humans body.

Iden himself didn't care as it were delicious to him! The fake one was not even a close match to it, and he would not drink that even if he died of thirst!

Jodran an ex-athlete waltzed over to him as soon as he entered the room. Tall, tanned, dirty blonde hair with weird yellow tinged eyes with a hint of red that showed he had been enjoying himself a little too well on the blood drinks that were available! Iden`s eyes had settled down now after his... blood binge. They were almost back to normal so now only hopefully Ashley were aware of his tumble into blood valley.

"What is the meaning of this meeting Iden?" Jodran shuffled up to him a bit close to comfort with the curious question. His odd eyes squinting side eyed at his only leader and waiting for answers.

"Time will tell Jodran." Iden said as he nodded in greeting. Not really that keen on the guy or wanting to be in his presence for too long. There was something about him that he did not like... Something about him that he did not trust. The same feeling that he had had with Fess, but had ignored until it were too late...

A couple in the room then saw that their leader had arrived and swiftly came over also to him as they pushed through the crowd.

Colin and Betty.

A couple who looked to be in their fifties that Iden very vaguely remembered were someone in his clans parents. He had not been best pleased that day years ago to learn that this bald slouched round man and his plump, grey already wife, were joining his clan as members fifty years ago or so.

He had doubted at the time that they could even soul collect without a walking stick, but they hadn't let him down on that one that even he were surprised by how faithful they were to the cause.

But due to their stubborn personalities he had had still found them a large home miles away from his own marvellous mansion like one. He had guessed that they would be the type of people to make pointless complaints at all hours for no reason at all but from mere boredom, and he wanted that as far away from him and his home as ex humanly possible.

After their turning on the same day there had been a lecture to his clan (minus them) a reminder that they could not just go around turning people into vamps willy nilly!

That there needed to be thought and careful reasoning behind it. Vampires needed to be strong, and by god most of them were beautiful or handsome and also, they must be deadly.

Mr and Mrs oddity as he liked to name them were as deadly as a dead donkeys aunt.

Colin tutted, "We were just settling down for the night Iden. This had better be important or I shall..." He swung his plump arms around.

"You shall what?" Iden's face changed into a spectacular force, and he glared at the male of the two with a harsh unfazed look to himself. He hastily grabbed a glass of blood from the side and sunk his fangs into it with a sighing pleasure. Groaning as he necked it in one.

He knew that he had to be careful with how much he drank as he had already over dosed on blood earlier that day. To continue on could be lethal.

To others.

"Nothing, nothing. Just we wanted an early night that is all." Colin looked like he were already regretting his spoken words to his leader and even his over bearing wife jabbed him hard in the side with an elbow to shut him up and stop him putting his foot in it any further.

"He`s our leader. Behave." She whispered to her mate in warning although whispering was rather pointless when you were in a large hall full of all hearing vampires. Luckily it seemed they were fated mates as well as ex human mates.

"Yes, Colin I am your leader." Iden grinned meanly at him pointedly. Colin scowled his way.

"Sorry." But not sounding sorry at all.

"And this is exactly why we only turn those in to vamps that can prove their worth. Turning o.a.p`s into vamps is strictly a no go." Iden looked at his nails bored. "Anyway..." He went to leave them. "I am off to do an announcement because you are not the only one that has a busy day tomorrow."

"Do you want me to come up there?" Ashley asked his leader sullenly. Not one for public speaking no, but he would do anything that his boss asked him to do.

Well mostly.

Iden shook his head to Ash as a firm no and continued up to the stage with no trepidation. He had no fear of this, no fear at all. He had been doing this speaking lark for hundreds of years and it meant nothing to him to have to speak in front of hundreds. Thousands.

He had been alive years longer as a vampire then the human that he ever were.

"Now can I have your attention please?" Iden said in a booming voice. No one looked. "Oi!" He yelled. Nope still nothing. They were all too busy catching up or moaning about being there to pay attention.

Iden went full on angry vamp. He threw his glass across the room, and he roared like an angry, demented lion that had sat on thorns.

Everyone stopped what they were doing.

"Why thank you." The fierce leader grinned out sarcastically. "Now I have your attention guys here is the deal. I will read out my list of problems for the evening and then wait for yours after that. We will go home, have a refresh, a sleep and a think and meet back tomm night."

"But I got a dinner date!" Yelled out one vamp. A thin, tanned skin vamp with a hooked nose called Creed, but who were all flawless except for that.

"Oh yeah, where's that then, cos it had better not be down on earth."

"No, no." The vamp said backtracking.

Clearly lying but not the balls to say it to their leader.

"Ok then. When you have finished lying, we shall begin." Iden spoke. "Problem one that I have. My brother has taken Ruby by force back to the darkness with him. We need to get her back soon and without fail before it is too late, and she will have to stay there. The longer she is in the darkness with him, the longer that she will be at risk of turning out like him sadly. Not very pleasant if you catch my drift." He added.

Then carried on, "Can someone come up with a plan that doesn't involve Ruby getting hurt and I suppose... My brother as well. Much."

There was shocked gasps and sighs and all the other vamps that knew her were outraged on Rubys behalf at being taken from that side of the realm into another. The ones that did not know her were just as sympathetic mainly.

Iden spoke clearly in a loud booming voice for them all to know.

"Problem two. Someone has been not doing their duty. On turning it is made very clear to you all that you are to soul collect in exchange for living the life of Riley up here. And eternal life - blah blah blah. One of you has not been soul collecting. This is the third time this week that it has happened at least and if it continues then the one responsible, shall find that soon they will be without a head as it will be separated by their body." He sighed. "Three and this is disturbing, but I hoped that it was merely rumour, but it now seems clearly not. There is two new members who are barely sixteen. I am not happy about this. Not happy at all. It is wrong, it is not right, and I would like to know the reason why they exist up here. Anyone? Anyone at all?"

Iden appeared to be able to go off like a bomb.

"I have seen them too." Colin said quietly with a strict gaze. His wife nodded in agreement and then spoke softly. "Me too. We saw them a week or so ago they were identical twins and with a man who I did not recognise from near ours. I just assumed that they were young looking but older vamps, if you get my drift..."

"No Betty. They are new vamps aged barely sixteen." Iden said in disgust.

"Jesus!" She muttered in horror. "I just thought... We had to leave the rest of our kids behind when we died and were reborn. We will outlive them which saddens me. We all know the rules though you are right. But they looked like dates though. Not their children or nothing..."

"Another Fess. But even sicker then." Colin spoke out in an angry show of words and was met by horror from around the room.

Iden totally agreed on that.

Who wouldn't? Fess had shamed the vampire realm with his actions. Now that someone else out there was doing the same.

"Crikey." Said Jodran. Even him as a player vamp would not touch a youngster with his bare claws.

"Crikey indeed. So now with problem three is that two teen females have been spotted. On dates." Iden emphasised the dates. He looked round the room, "And not as I suspected as someone`s children that they have rescued from the human world after death which might have been forgivable but as someone`s dates..."

He growled and he struggled to keep the monster within his body. But maybe showing just a hint of the monster would prove them whoever it were not to mess with him. But not everyone were there in the clan for they would not all fit in; some would be asleep or working or maybe avoiding the meeting entirely!

There was that many that it was difficult to keep stock of every one in his clan though he probably should keep tabs!

But with new members added and a few here and there destroyed it quite frankly were.

Too hard.

"Right, that is me done then. Shall we go over? Saving Ruby, someone not soul collecting and illegal teen turning. That wraps it up."

"Would it be allowed if they were eighteen?" A vamp with a mohawk nearby called out.

"Yes." Said Iden. "But not just to be fawned around and used as – dates." He hissed that. He eyed the speaker in an unpleasant way and decided to keep an eye on that specific person from then on in also. The list seemed to be increasing. "Now does anyone have any other issues?" He asked.

The room was silent but then –

"I...I do...."

"Yes. Um... Dorothy, wasn't it?"

"Yes sir." She said meekly. She reminded him of Ruby in a small way. Small build, dark hair in braids but he knew that she had been around nearly as long as he had. But it still seemed even then wasn't long enough to bring her out of her shyness for it was just her sweet and gentle personality. "My chosen mate of many years my husband, has just met his...urgh fated mate."

Heads swung to look at her old man. Wow Iden were not expecting that! All eyes stared still stared at her husband. This was not an event that had ever really occurred.

A chosen mate and a fated one!

"I see." He gritted. "And you. Edgar, isn't it?"

"Sir. I want to stay with Dorothy but I urm... I don't know if I can leave. Her." He whispered in a daze, meaning his other mate. He was also one of the older ones with straight auburn hair and muscley arms.

"Well, you are going to have to darlin for she is not coming here!" Snapped Dorothy uncharitably. Glowering at her poor husband.

"But my sweet!"

"No, you listen here. NO! She will not be one of us I will see that she doesn't. If you want her so bad, you will have to leave here after hundreds of years together...." She pointed at her aghast husband. She shed a tear and wept dramatically. He tried to wipe it from his loving wife's cheek, but she turned away in distress with her braids swinging to the side.

She looked a bit like Wednesday Addams.

You could tell by the atmosphere in the room that Edgar was being hated on by nearly all that were there. They were chosen mates. Dorothy and Edgar. Edgar and Dorothy. They came as a pair like chalk and cheese and had done before anyone could remember when they weren't as one.

Until the pull of the fated mate bond that were.

Iden butted in on the two rowing amongst themselves. If he did not, then he would likely be there all night and he was fucking tired of it all.

"Enough."

He looked around the room For Greggory who to his surprise were there at the back of the room.

"Geoffrey?" He barked at him.

He clapped his hands in order.

"Boss." He scuttled over like the crab from the little mermaid.

"Tell all here in this room about the mate bond as I know most here have not faced it for themselves yet. Geoffrey here has finally had the pleasure of finding his fated mate and he is going to live with her on earth. Urm Susan wasn't it? Kinda surprised he is still here to be honest but pleased that he can tell about his bonded one."

For now, Iden knew exactly what it meant to meet your own one and only. Heck, he was only in that meeting now that the reasons keeping him there were far too important to be ignored for a time!

"It is like being two magnets pulled together. Not wanting to be apart from each other. The draw of the mate bond will tie us two together until the very bitter end." Geoffrey gasped out in a mad fluster. His round cheeks blushed as he swooned over his love who could not be with him that day. "She does not want to die as of yet, so I am going to live there. Goodbye everyone! I will see you soon." He waved cheerily in an overly happy manner.

No one would be sad to see him go but the way that he acted they would all be in tears at his imminent departure.

Choosing to pick the rustle and bustle of the human world where only Susan and fellow vamps could see him then to force her to become a vampire like him and to live in the hidden realm with him.

Clearly a braver man then most. Or a more stupider one.

Iden rolled his eyes at the feeble goodbyes then smiled grimly. His lips stiffened. "Now sickening as that is hearing that from old Geoffrey here. It is true what he said. As I met my own fated one today. Elfina." He gasped out her name as it still made him breathless even just to hear it.

Now it was his time to have all eyes on him as he spoke speedily so that time would speed by. "It is indescribable. And the fact that only she could see me after hundreds of years of being unseen in the human

world on my visits there. All I could describe it was as simply... wow. As
is she."

There was cheers around the room and whoop – whoops as his
loyal subjects congratulated him and Geoffrey on finding what it was,
they had been looking for.

Him mainly...Iden.

"Silence everyone." They shut up begrudgingly as Iden scowled.
"Now Dorothy. What do you think now you have dealt with the harsh
reality of the fated mate bond that no doubtfully your husband has? I
sympathise with your plight, I really do. But as you have heard the mate
bond out ways anything else besides. I myself got pulled back to soul
collecting and then here in only a short amount of time of meeting my
one and only."

"Diddum's." Said Dorothy to Iden in a heartless manner with a
shrug.

"I will cut his head off his shoulders before I let her have him."

"Go on then for I know that you won't."

And before Iden could respond to that she had grabbed a large
sword that must have belonged to her husband and cut his head clean
off there on the spot. The head of her husband clanged as the sword hit
the flesh and then it fudded onto the bare floor at her high heeled feet.

Shit.

"If I can't have him then no one can." Yelled Dorothy stomping
her foot and wriggled in two muscular vampire guards arms who had
moved the sword a safe distance away from the irate woman and had
held her, so she did not attack further. Although most guessed that now
her husband was gone that, that was the end to her slaughtering spree
that night.

A female voice yelled in agreement, "Hear, hear!" Cheered Justina
who had obviously snuck in unaware just in time to hear and to see
Dorothy decapitate her husband.

His ex-lover glared straight at Iden who decided to hot foot it out of there.

"Someone clean that up." Iden said pointing at the lone head that would forever have a shocked expression on its poor face. Pretending that he had not seen Justina or her two cronies at the back of the room.

Accompanied by Corsa- a red headed beauty. Small slightly plump with a very large chest like a red headed Dolly Parton.

And Drokna – Chinese, dark hair and freckles. Lean and tall.

When the three were together they were likely up to something.

Something against him if Justina got to them.

Had she heard him tell all about Elfina? He wasn't sure truthfully. "I will deal with you at a later date." He pointed a finger roughly at the tearful Dorothy who was seemingly now then regretting losing her temper all of a sudden and ending her poor not yet unfaithful, husbands life.

Then he left.

Thanking fuck that the meeting were over.

CHAPTER EIGHT

I DEN
   The next day Iden returned to the human world in the afternoon after lunch as the sun reached its burning peak. He had been so eager to get back to his one that he hadn't slept well at all the night previously. Waiting until day light hit but then getting caught up in major realm business to be able to go down to be with her any earlier than that.

Dorothy would have to be sentenced.

He knew that.

Either by himself or by a higher being if he handed her over to the judgement realm for sentencing. They did not just deal with judging humans there but all else in between. They did not like to. For many humans died each day. Many souls came through their wide-open doors each day.

He betted that she would get away with killing her poor defenceless husband that she had carelessly, ok- brutally murdered in front of a chunk of the clan it was not him dealing out the punishment. To lose two soul collectors in rapid times would put the soul collecting back a notch so she would likely be spared a death sentence by those higher up.

He just wondered what Edgar`s fated mate would think on her fated mate never returning to her. Never seeing him again. For no one would tell her of his death and she wouldn't see them if they did try to tell her what had happened.

To prevent her own un- happiness, Dorothy had caused someone else`s eternal doom. More than one.

Iden swooped down to where he had left Elfina the day before. Luckily for him soul collecting had been rather slow that day.

Did no one want to die that day? Maybe luck were finally shining out like a diamond on him. Maybe it were a coincidence though. He just hoped that he did not get the call when he was with her again like he had previously. There was things he needed to say first before that happened.

Things he needed to do.

Like her...

He knocked on the door of the flat impatiently and waited for an answer. To his surprise and displeasure, the shop she owned next door were shuttered tightly shut and it looked like it had been that way all day from what he could sense. Her scent was noon existent there as though all traces of it had blown away in the wind.

What had happened to Elfina? He felt uneasy. He never felt that way.

The door opened with a creek.

Iden became a monster again as a strange man dared to open the door to his mates home with no qualms at being there.

"Mine!" He yelled which only brought confusion on the sneering man's face as he would likely not have heard it.

He knew that she were his and him hers. This guy. Who was he? He were no one. Noone at all.

"Who's there?" The man leant forward but seeing no one there he then paused and made to shut the door as though half wanting to keep it open and half wanting to keep it shut tight.

Iden flitted through the open door after closing his wings to get into the tight space without the man feeling it. He followed him up the stairs. Wanting to push him down them.

Had she left him? Given up her own home to another to get away from him and his abnormalities? No, he was adamant that she felt the pull of the bond as strongly, as purely, just like he had. And when he gave her his own essence and he took hers then the mate bond would be complete, and they would be forever as one.

The man sat back on the sofa where it looked like he had been sleeping and making himself at home. While he sat there dozing off, Iden crept quietly around the flat looking for traces of Elfina. His mate. Her scent was low, so it appeared that she had not been there since the day before that. So again, question was, who was that man hiding out in her flat?

What did he want?

He did not smell like her kin, and Iden were fully aware from Ruby`s stories that she had told before he learnt that she was his mates sister that they had no one anyway.

Iden then saw it.

The letter. Hmm. Interesting... He looked over mysteriously across the flat to make sure that the strange dozing man, was not looking his way right then and picked it up with sure fingers in one swoop. It looked to have been well read from what he could tell.

He sensed there was no cameras in the flat only leading to it and in the very heart of the shop, but he wanted to do everything right so that it was not known that he were there by anyone unwanted.

No way to tell he had been. He didn't want to frighten Elfina anymore then he had to do. He would rather die than that! He knew the frazzled man could not see him for sure unless he were some kind of miracle, but he would see the letter being lifted with no hand in thin air, if Iden lifted it at the wrong possible moment in time!

He felt nerves creeping as he read it swiftly his eyes, glancing at the small, scribbled page. Fury took over him in a mere instant as he read it again and again, but he tried to remain calm and non-irate. He looked around her desk quietly as come be, as silent as a small mouse with tiny feet.

Sifting through, finding more evidence in her desk, police reports, news cut outs, more letters as he sifted through it all with his blood boiling as he went through it.

A file full of evidence. A mug shot. Karl. The guy on the chair. He was Karl. He was her stalker.

Well not anymore! If he had a pulse in ten minutes, he would be one lucky fella!

The guys phone rang, and the stranger guy who was now named answered it with relative ease. His voice were as dishevelled as his looks were then appearing like a total slime ball, "Hello? Oh, hi mate. Yes, I am just dealing with business at the moment in the city. I am at Elfina`s now. Yep, there will be no getting away from me this time that I tracked her down again!" The guy sniggered. "Going to make her come back with me! Kinda was getting fed up with her breaking free from me over and over." He laughed throatily. "Ok will do." He hung up the phone with a firm click.

Not realising that the words he had spoken would likely be the death of him.

As the call quickly ended, Iden saw red for danger. His eyes if they could be seen by others right then were red as can be. The darkest red possible. He threw himself at the surprised man who was even more confused by what were happening and grabbed him by the scruff of his skinny neck roughly as come be.

"What's going on? What's happening to me?" The man screamed in his fear at being grabbed by no one.

No one at all. Soon he would find out what real fear were. Iden would guarantee it. He would ensure it. If he didn't then what sort of vampire would he be?

He hauled the kicking out at him man, to the large window in the lounge with ease as he were half his size and threw him with all his might straight through it, the glass shattered totalling the window completely into nothing.

As the man fell harshly down to the ground from the first floor like a sack of spuds, the murdering vamp curiously peered through the now large break in the window that took it nearly all up, having in all his years never have pushed anyone through a pane of glass, and watched in fascination as the stalker Karl man, now lay splatted on the ground below.

His eyes hauntingly open – sightless, and his nose seeping with blood.

It made Iden feel good to see his corpse laid there, it made him feel sane to see that he had avenged Elfina with the vile mans end of time. He could only imagine the fear that she must have felt being pursued over and over by this reckless man time and time again, not listening to the word no and having to move to get away from him and his deranged fantasies of them being together forever.

But now thanks to the vampire clan leader, justice was served. Karl would not be chasing anyone again unless he miraculously came to life which were unlikely. Instead, he would be chased by the punishers in the lower realms for all of eternity...

Iden liked that.

Knowing as he had seen cameras in the downstairs hall that he could not leave through the front door as it would be seen opening with no help from a person, so he pushed himself through the huge break in the window and he jumped as high as come be into the nighttime air.

As he spiralled down to the ground clutching his swords as his marvellous black wings opened to catch him safe and sound, he hit the ground on his two feet not a mark on his body.

He walked over, spiting at Karl`s corpse that were mangled on the ground where he belonged. Beneath them.

Not even tempted to touch that scum bags blood with his bare fangs, even though he thirsted for it more than life itself.

Instead, only craving the blood of the innocent – his Elfina. He would have to let her know that he accidentally, ok on purpose maybe, hurled what it appeared were her stalker through her lounge window and down to his eventual death.

Would she be pleased or pissed with him he asked himself? He did not know the answer to that.

Time would tell. The sirens of the help that would be too late came five minutes later, and neighbours came bustling around to see what had happened and about who they had seen out the corner of their eyes take a furious fumble out of the first storey window with his arm splayed. Was he pushed or did he throw himself the busy bodies muttered to and fro?

Someone shielded their children's gaze from the vile man's corpse ok Iden felt a little guilty at that one as to him children were merely innocents after all...

But in Iden`s opinion Karl got everything that he had deserved now he knew who he really were.

She was his!

How dare the weak mortal try and take his all-time love away from him!

He paused silently pondering and tried to concentrate on what had to be done, tried to send a signal through to the judgement realm that there was a soul for collection and no collector, but he could not get through.

Probably ignoring him!

The longer he lay there the longer that he was tempted to bit into his thick neck and take what was owed to him. For messing with his one and only. Should he, shouldn't he?

Before he could think twice, he bit hard into the stalkers body and only stopped when someone came running over to where it lay. He spat onto the wound- hiding the evidence of his fangs.

Still no word from the other realm.

So, he sighed in annoyance and picked up the recently murdered soul in his reluctant arms before it became aimless, nameless and he took it on its way – its way to hell. Leaving its body lying on the ground. That would not be needed. He had taken what were needed.

But first he had to stop off quickly. For as said before, sadly it was not his choice to make.

He approached the judgement realm and entered the main chambers in long, impatient strides. He put his wings firmly down behind his thick back and glanced around for someone to help him there, so that he did not have to stop off long with this frightful soul that only deserved the fiery pits of the lower realm.

He knew that his own brother simply throwed the soul through the door of the judgement realm and ran. It was why they never bumped into each other. He preferred to make sure the recently lost one had been signed in before he went on his way.

This realm in were now in was not that big. He approached the main room and threw the stalking soul down on the floor in a mangled heap. Not giving it his usual care that he liked to give his souls.

"Hey, any service round here?" He called out impatiently at one of the desks with a loud impatient tut. He didn't have all day, did he!?

There was somewhere he had to be. Someone he had to see. To be with. Forever. In eternal peace and harmony.

He huffed and tapped his boots impatiently onto the cool floor. As usual the room they were now in was filled with at least a few hundred desks in which someone sat behind most of them checking souls in for their judgement. Some were occupied by souls on the other side, others weren't.

The room was silent but at other times loud.

"Coming, coming." A beady, bald as a coot, little man with smart brown glasses came rushing over to that specific desk in front of an impatient Iden, as fast as he could go on his relatively short legs. "Oh, it's you." He said as the man saw that it were Iden at the front desk awaiting him and not someone better.

A soul at his feet. But not his to keep. If it were and it was, he would see that it would spend all its day in pure and utter torture that weakened the mind and tore the soul. He hoped that it would.

"Charming." Iden spoke this rather dryly. "Pleasure to see you too judger. What was your name again?" He asked this with a raised dark brow as though he had no idea at all.

"Victor." Iden knew it really, he must do for he was one of the eternals like this man at the desk were! They had bumped into each other on many, many occasions. But Iden could not imagine spending an eternity in that place with all those ungrateful ones that came in there for judgement!

"Ok, I have a few questions for the computer." The man Victor said as he quickly typed with fast, fat fingers.

Iden nodded. He knew the routine. Of course, he did. It was like being at the checkout in Aldi. They had to be super-fast because they needed to be.

"Do you know how he died?" Victor asked Iden. The soul had now awakened and gasped and wiggled on the ground next to them both like a slimy worm hanging on a hook. Looking around the plain white room with amazement on its startled face and opening its mouth like a guppy.

"Am I dead?" It asked Iden with a gasp and a shudder, interrupting Victor who were now getting impatient with them. Soon there would be other souls needed to check in. To learn their fate. There was no time to dawdle. No time to waste.

"Yes, thank fuck." Iden drawled out now bored and rolled his eyes at the nuisance on the floor who no longer had a body.

The soul annoyingly started to speak, "Why is there lots of dwarf`s here? I must be dreaming!" Karl could see them all now all those that had been hidden from him now that he had passed, and they were now all visible to him.

Only seeing what were desired of him.

"Hey, have some respect. These guys here are more men then you ever were or could be." Iden pointed a sharp claw at the thankfully dead fucker who was at the right place. At his feet. Shamefully not squashed under them like a mere slimy bug.

"Were?" A shocked gasp from the soul. Gasps lit the room as the other souls around the room all realised a similar thing. The sound was clenching on ones ears.

"Yes, were." Iden gritted his oh so perfect, pearly teeth, and tried not to lose his cool anymore then he already had that night. The guy was dead, dead as a dodo so it could not get that much worse for him. Plus, he would never lay eyes on Elfina again.

Ever.

"I was waiting for Elfina and then..."

"Do not say her name!" Iden boomed out loudly with a fierce demanding order. Karl winced in fright and backed down from talking any further to the monster before him. Too cowardly to fight for what he deemed to be his woman.

Which she never were. Never would be.

Iden would kill him again and again and again until his soul were no more before that ever happened in his lifetime.

Victor eyed them wearily, not sure who was more bothersome – the grim soul on the floor or the vampire that had put him there.

"Cause of death? Do u know it? Not being rude here but I have other many, many poor souls to check in. There being more souls then judgers to check them in here."

"Yes. He fell through a first-floor window. Faceplanted the floor. Possibly needs a nose job if he didn't already!" Iden looked away shiftily and shuffled his feet as Victor studied him with narrowed eyes. They were well acquainted with each other clearly. Victor knew all his faults as Iden knew all Victors perfection.

It was why one was a vamp, and one was a judger.

"Quite. Cause of death please?" Victor peered through his specs impatiently.

"I threw him through it." Iden`s said straight faced. Deadly serious.

"Hey!" Karl cried outraged. "You killed me! That's not on!"

Silence.

Then – "You threw him through a window? Killing him. You know you will get written up for that. We will be in touch with your punishment. Ok, you can go now. Unless there is anything else that you need to...confess?" Victor said this scratching his bald head as he ordered another little person, a hot, red headed woman, to take the soul away for judgment with a polite nod.

Iden turned, "Yeah. But be warned what`s ya face. If he gets send to the higher realm or I see his face again anytime what so ever in my lifetime, then I will drag him to the lower realm myself and chain him there. Got it?"

"And this is why we recommend you vamps drop them off at the door. Snarly, aggressive blood suckers."

"You had better believe it." Iden winked.

Karl was now having his finger print done across the room before he left. The red headed lady firmly at his side. She were small but still she were very pretty.

As his print were taken an alarm sounded loudly blaring out, and a beacon shone out bright red. Across the way a hundred or so souls being checked in looked round sluggishly to see what the noise were and where it were coming from. If they did not hurry, there would be a blockage as more and more souls were brought in one by one, two by two, as if they were queuing for Noah's ark...

But they weren't.

They would either be spending forever doing pleasurable things or having bad things done to them. Some guessed it yet others were oblivious to it.

"Hmm. Well, his finger print sent the sound alarm off, so I think we have no chance of him going to anywhere but the lower realm. But it's not my decision to make. We have his file ready on the system. Take him away." Victor clicked his finger at the other little man who came on by and looked a bit like Clark Kent who helped Karl away through another door and took over from the red head.

She seemed to work at the finger print station.

As soon as Karl were out of there Iden left in a shot. Ignoring one of the punishers having a crafty fag outside of the building, holding it in his clawed grip, right next to a no smoking sign that stated – no smoking please, punishers that means you.

You did not want to looked them green beasts straight in the eye and even vampires knew not to do that unless they were down for a brutal fight that could go on and on while time whizzed by. Iden thought that the punishers looked like a cross between a lizard and an ogre with scaled skin, claws and the most oddest face ever.

Some were humanoid like, but others were monster faced, That one chain smoking by the door one was more monster face in the shape of an alligator with small sharp teeth and bulging eyes.

Iden had only been in a fight with one once – never again, if he could so help it. He had been lucky to have kept his head intact at the end of it.

The guy had tried to take a chunk out of his arm also.

If humans knew what met them down in the lower realm, he bet that they would think twice about their misdemeanours on earth when they were alive then!

"Prick." Iden muttered to Karl although he were long gone as he went on his way. Unleashing his vivid wings and flying away fast from the punishers lizard like gaze, that scored through the back of him as he flew.

CHAPTER NINE.

E LFINA - EARLIER

Elfina ran as fast as her sturdy legs would possibly take her. Relieved that she had her bank card and bag on her person, or else she would have been royally screwed right about then. She had an idea sing to her as she wondered what to do and so took her and Sniggles to the Maids head Hotel, a short walk away but not to close that Karl could know where she were.

Ten minutes or so a walk from her home. Wearing pjs, trainers and a coat!

She had been there before when she had first eagerly arrived in the old, great city of Norwich, and she had needed to get her things sorted out quick and she from her previous visit knew it would be pet friendly for an extra charge.

Somewhere then for her to lay her head down and to think about what to do for the night ahead. She had after all seen a god damned invisible man!

Built like a prince, with wings. A hot one at that.

She checked in, luckily, they had a room available in which she nearly cried tears of happiness and they didn't seem to find it odd too much what she were wearing and then held Sniggles tightly in her arms and made a quick but important call.

He wiggled in her arms. Not liking change and not liking that she had taken him out late at night and she had forgotten his toys.

He were a nervous dog. But hers.

At the moment she completely understood that. Her own fear was getting to her too and her heart raced as though she had run a marathon.

Two rings of the phone then a sudden answer – "Hello?"

"Oh, Lovella it's you!" Elfina breathed a sigh of relief and gasped at hearing her friends voice. She whispered to someone next to her.

"Elfina whatever is the matter?" Lovella asked, sounding worried. "We were worried about you earlier you were acting... weird. Seeing somebody...who wasn't there."

Well, there goes her telling her about her winged, handsome hero who had flown off into the night without a trace who she had pined for a kiss from, Elfina thought to herself sadly.

"I`m ok. Karl is at mine, he not long turned up. I took the dog and legged it from there! We are at the Maid`s head Hotel. I did not know where else to be..."

"He what?" Lovella sounded outraged.

"Yeah, I know. I`m laying low."

"Laying low? It is your flipping flat he's in. What if he trashes the place? Ring the police! Or else I will go round and tear him a new..."

"No, no." Elfina shook her head and put down the dog. He sat at her feet loyally like the good Sniggles he could be, and he watched the door for other dogs with interest.

His ears pricking in interest as he saw people walk swiftly past into the dead of the night. Elfina knew that she had to hurry up with the call as If her fidgety dog saw another dog, he would be off out of there like a shot, and she couldn't have that.

Nor could she carry him and hold the heavy phone stuck to the wall at the same time. "Karl wouldn't do that. If he is there tomorrow, I will call them, I promise."

"Promise?" Lovella whispered to someone again. "Megan asks if you are alright. Do you need us to come? Imogen went home not long after you."

"No, its fine honestly. I will contact you when I get back tomorrow."

She hung up the call and took the twitching dog swiftly up the flight of stairs to her room.

After getting in she settled him down and snuck downstairs to get them both something to eat. She took it to her room, fed the dog and snuggled up with him to watch the last and end part of Manifest that made her weep.

Then after while waiting for the next day to begin she fell blissfully asleep.

Twelve hours later of dozing in and out of consciousness in her oh, so cozy bed, she begrudgingly got up and made to leave the nice hotel with Sniggles as he should - by her side. She checked out of there pronto and had a gentle walk around the block.

She had brought some leggings and a floaty purple top in a nearby store so that she didn't attract gawps and stares from her pjs.

Darn you Karl she hissed to herself at each purchase that hit her bank balance.

Plucking up the courage to leave for home but not quite getting there as of yet. For what awaited her at her home was someone that she had moved across to the city from. Who had blighted her life with endless pop ups, bumping into`s and communications that she did not want or need.

After a few hours of passing nerves, she took the short, scary walk towards her home. As she walked down her road, she saw it pop out in front of her view– a body on the side walk in front.

What!

Her heart pounded in her chest with a great extent. What had happened here she wondered? She put the wiggling again dog down and waited behind the police line with impatience.

Who had died there? She could see a body kind of but could not make them out. Nor did she want to. Police were everywhere, it were crawling with them so it must have happened close to her home she so guessed.

"Elfina!" She spun round at the sound of a voice.

His.

Wow.

She shivered in desire. Shivered in anticipation. No, no, no! What was wrong with her she scolded herself, there was a blooming corpse on the nearby floor on the sidewalk.

Hardly romantic, was it? No, it wasn't but she couldn't help feeling that way just by seeing him again there.

"Iden!" She screeched as she saw him appear from out of thin air. Blushing of her cheeks, then a sincere smile. Fuck he looked good.

She bet he always did...

A nosing old lady, one of her neighbours across the road with a blue rinse nearby looked at her with a sharp frown.

"Are you talking to me, dearie?" When someone said dearie, it always reminded her of the show – once upon a time.

"No, no sorry. I was talking to him!" Elfina held her hands out in apology and smiled at the confused lady sincerely. Then remembering that the old lady couldn't see Iden either. If she did, she would have been in for a treat.

"Hmmm." The old lady gave her an odd look then looked back towards the police with urgent interest that would not sway.

She had a thought that could go either way, "Could you watch my dog for me? Please. I live over there but can't go in there due to that. I won't be long." Elfina pointed in the direction of the corpse who was then being put away into a body bag and prepared to go.

"There. Where the man fell? That flat? Oh dearie of course I can. Take all the time you need and then some." The snotty old lady turned on the charm and swept Sniggles up into her arms and snuggled him tight like he were a teddy.

Sniggles looked miffed and then snuggled himself into the ladies arms.

"The... the flat?" She looked up and then looked over to her lovely home that may still contain her stalker and it suddenly hit her – the body had fallen straight from her own bloody flat!

Who? What? Why?

Was it Karl? Should she feel bad for hoping that out of anyone it would be someone like him for he deserved it. But in her life, she had only ever seen the good taken away, and the bad ones that remained.

She ran hurriedly over to Iden after tearing her eyes from her precious dog and discretely guided Iden out of the way. For although only she could see him, she did not want to look like she were there talking to himself in front of all the emergency crew for fear of being carted away in a strait jacket, in the back of a nearby ambulance.

"Iden. Iden!" She hissed to him quietly. He looked at her from head to toe as though she was all his favourite chocolate bars rolled into in one. He stepped nearer to her, so she was a breath apart from him.

Still too far.

She shuddered. He smelt so good, and she wanted to kiss him, kiss him again, possibly do more so fucking much more that words could not say!

"Yes, my one?" He beamed at her in awe and all the anger that she felt deep inside, the stress and the tiredness, all the misunderstanding over the past few days it all faded away into- into... well nothing.

"Karl is dead. You need no fear anymore my sweet one." He cupped her face with a gentle hand that soothed her to no fault as he caressed it. His touch brought a gentle urgency to her.

She wanted this man there. Man, beast, whatever he truly were. For the face that she had seen the day before she had only seen a glimpse but had known that it was not a human one.

It couldn't be. No human looked like that, and she had seen him chop and change from perfection into something quite deadly.

She looked at him with her stunned eyes. If she would die that very day, then that was the face that she would only want to see because he was beautiful.

"You sure? Why, what happened to him? Did you...." She wrung her hands in front of herself and looked nervous by it. As much as she hoped and prayed that Karl was at last not of this earth, the mere thought of someone's death being at her hand made her feel guilt unlike nothing she had ever felt before.

Had he killed for her? But then it was a dog-eat-dog world out there.

"That I did." She barely heard him as he uttered it quietly. But she knew what she had heard. Even if it was said in a husky whisper, it was the sound of a confession.

"But why?" She fluttered her eyes and sighed, touched his toned, firm arm, the arm of an apparent killer but she needed to know, she wanted to know what had happened back in her home. What had led to the death of her stalker at the hands of this fine man before her.

One that she had wished for previously. But now that it had arisen, she did not know what she truly felt.

Before she could think or act any further, he picked her up in his large comforting arms and he took her away from there with great speed. His magnificent wings spun out fully wide and he then flew them both to the top of a multi-story car park where he placed her down carefully away from the danger of the edge.

She yelped in astonish.

She then whirled around and hit out at him with her hands. "Why did you?"

"Sit here with me please. And then I will tell you everything. Will you be by my side and listen to me, my Elfina?"

"Always." She nodded as though her body were now a puppet and she would obey his every command.

He pointed to the floor at the edge of the car park up top. They were now on the roof of the building and this part was away from anyone hopefully over hearing them speak.

"Elfina I was alive once much like you. But I died. My brother brought me back as one of the living dead. Vampires we are called by you humans."

She scoffed in disbelief.

"Yeah, right ok then.... Next you will tell me that Santa Claus is your dad and Mrs Claus is your mum!"

He smiled but it did not reach his eyes as though her simple remark had hurt him in ways that she did not yet understand. "My parents are a long time dead, Elfina. They have been dead many years my one. My sister she is also long gone. It is only me and my elder brother Rhys who is the one that turned me that are still alive, although we have no heartbeat to call our own no more, we are still here." He paused and then continued on before she could saddle him with questions.

"My dad did look a bit like Santa, but my mother... fuck she was beautiful."

Elfina looked as if she did not know what to say to that but then she tilted her pretty head back and laughed in what could only be described as a loud giggle. "Yes ok, vampires! Ha de ha!" She guffawed again. "Vampires! Grunting.

"It is true." Iden held her hands softly with his over them, bringing one up to his lips to kiss it. "I will prove it to you but just know this. I would rather end my life now than to ever hurt you."

"Well show me then. Vamp." She did not seem to believe him, that he must know. Now Iden would know how Geoffrey felt as he had also to take that step before.

As she looked at the handsome face of the dark-haired man by her mere side, she then saw a glimpse of what she had seen yesterday pass a shadow over his face. His face changed into something else, and his teeth grew into sharp impressive fangs that looked as though they could bite straight through her very flesh.

His hands turned into startling claws as his nails vanished into sharpened points. She gasped in shock but not an ounce of fear as he brushed a claw against her cheek, whilst being careful not to mark her with it.

She as her heart thudded and her suspicions now grew placed her hands onto his bulky chest. She scrunched her nose as it wrinkled as she then come to the realisation that this man in front of her – this possible vampire, did not have a heartbeat of his own.

Did hers beat for both of them?

She grabbed his wrist and her clammy fingers felt for a pulse, there must be one, there must! – but as she suspected now – there was none. She looked down at his flat and toned stomach and then back at his kissable lips and there was no in or out of his chest to speak of and no air escaped or entered his hot, silky mouth as he moved it.

He was no mortal. But he was alive...

He leant into her. "There is none. I do not breath, my chest does not beat Elfina, even for you although I want it too. I have eternal life, for I do not need these to now live."

"But how?" In silent answer to this his face turned back into a human like one that melted his harsh monster like features into more pleasant to look at ones.

"The story is long, but I would like you to still be here at the end, if you can stomach it to be here at the end of it." He grinned.

"I will try." She said with one of her sweet smiles that pulled at his cold chest. But she knew either way that she would still be there even if it was not what she wanted to hear.

For she had to be.

Dark and mysterious eyes met her more human ones, "I am one of the first few vampires. My brother, he died, but me and my family did not know that – he just disappeared, never to return!" A heavy feeling grew in Elfina's stomach at the mention of someone disappearing.

For it had happened to her with her sister...

"When I died, he appeared out of the blue and brought me back to life, and so I became just like him. One of the earlier vampires. We are also soul collectors. We instinctively know when we need to collect a soul – you remember me spacing out last night? That was a time that I had to go off and collect. In exchange for soul collecting for an anonymous higher being, we are given the gift of eternal life. Nothing can kill us except for decapitation or being burnt to ashes, we do not age either, inside or out."

"But...but..."

"Let me finish. Then speak how you feel free." He put out a hushing hand to her. She nodded in gentle agreement, liking it when he were dominating of her.

"We can survive on little food; we can survive on little blood although we crave it. But if we go for long periods of time without it then we are more than quite likely to go feral and to try to get it in any way that we possibly can. When I am stressed, I crave it more than a human may crave the thirst of water."

"Do you crave my blood?" She asked him quietly. But she wanted him to. She did not know why but she wanted him to. She could imagine him thirsting on her, being quenched with her. It did not frighten her in any way. In fact, it made her feel – hot and bothered with it.

Flustered even.

He gulped and sniffed into the air as he smelt her sudden scent that then arose from her. He smelt that she were becoming aroused, and he could then smell the blood that ran through her veins as if it ran through his own body.

He hesitated - then he nodded. "More than anything."

"Then bite me." She pulled down the collar on her recently born outfit so that he could get a glimpse of her slender, perfect neck. He looked away as his fangs grew yet again into monstrous ones and he licked his lips in what could only be- gentle wanting of her.

And what she contained.

"I cannot." He pulled back from her enticing smell and flesh. Fear in his eyes.

A car interrupted them as it drove past, and they stopped and waited for it to leave. The passengers looked at Elfina sitting alone on the car park roof with a frown and then turned round and continued on with family life.

"I want to feel what it is like. I want you to suck the goodness from my soul." She said with complete and utter honesty. Before she could finish her pleading sentence, he were on her in a speedy flash. He grabbed her hard and brought his wet lips to her, and they had a sweet, soul-destroying kiss that she never wanted to end as long as she so lived.

Then she whined as he pulled away and plunged his fangs straight into her willing, offered neck. He traced his fingers lightly down to her panties delving underneath, and plunged one into her, and then two, followed by three. He fingered her fast and touched her clit at the same time with his thumb like a pro as he sucked her blood hard with a ravenous pull.

She to no surprise came hard with a gush in no time at all as he finally stopped feasting on her now truly satisfied.

He pulled away.

Her blood still lingered there on his lips. His eyes grew red from his fullness.

"That was the most delicious thing that I have ever tasted. And I have been drinking blood for more time then I care to admit." He said huskily. She blushed at the thought of being fingered in a car park by a random guy – ok, a vamp, that she did not hardly know, she had felt like she did. But that she knew – he owned her. As she no doubtfully owned him. "Your pussy was so wet for me. Mmm. You enjoyed it, didn't you?"

She simply nodded and he groaned in untouched pleasure.

He swept her into his strong arms and held her tightly, his fingers still clearly wet from her juices. Pulling her onto his lap so that she was safe in his hold.

His invisible hold.

"Time is short. I must continue the story before we go any further." He seemed sullen all of a sudden. The change in his mood was noticeable.

"Yes, yes, I would like that. And thank you. That was very... enjoyable." She fidgeted in earnest on his enclosed lap.

"My pleasure. So on with the story as I do need to get back home."

"And where is home? I cannot believe that there are vampires roaming the earth. It is eerie..." She was feeling over whelmed. At ill ease that there may be vampires out there more dangerous than he. Because she was an avid reader. She knew what vampires were supposed to be like as they roamed through her books.

He instantly shook his head. "The earth is not our home. Well not on the ground as you know it. We are like birds; we soar up high into the sky – where the vampire realm lies. Some vampires are earth dwellers but most, nearly all are realm dwellers. There is three realms – the judgment realms. Here is where souls are taken by us to be judged. It is usually a quick process as everything that has been done on earth is recorded so they are aware of how good or bad they have been in their lifetime."

"Wow...."

Where would she go, she asked herself? She hadn't been that bad in life, had she? Although Karl had apparently been killed due to her. But he deserved it. Didn't he? Yep! He did!

The words flowed off his tongue as he had told the same story over and over before, "Yes... wow. From there the soul is placed in the higher realms – a heaven like place or the lower realms – what you would class as hell. The vampire realm is up where the judgment realm is and can only be seen by blood takers and all animals."

"Where has Karl gone?"

"Oh, most likely hell." His eyes twinkled.

She eyed him curiously. "So, I would not be able to see this... realm that you call home?"

"No, lass. Not quite yet."

"So, if you are up there." She pointed, "And I am down here." She gestured with a finger. "How do we date? See each other... That is if you wanted to that is...."

"You are not my date. You are my mate, my fated one. It was Ruby who led me to you in fact my love."

"Ruby! Where is she, tell me she is ok...?" Her words coming out of her mouth a million miles an hour.

He smiled which only made his handsome face all the more beautiful to her, he took her breath away,"She is like me, Elfina. She was dying and I made her like me. I am sorry but it was the only way to save her... I could not let her die...I just couldn't..."

"No, no, thank you!" She flung her arms around him in a heartbeat and snuggled into him as the tears fell from her face. She did not bother to hide her tears from him. He deserved to see the happiness that he had brought her from saving her sister.

Her despair over his sister being replaced with something – with hope. "Can I see her? Oh, I guess if she is like you then I can`t see her." Her face dropped in her sorrow as she remembered that her sister would be hidden from her view. She spaced out as she remembered the singing in the shop – it was her!

"Was that her in my shop?"

"Aye. And also, aye. Vampires to let us do our soul work peacefully and to keep our realm a secret it must remain invisible to any human eyes. The only ones that can see us our those in the other realms and our one and only human mate. You are my human mate that is why you can see me. You and you alone are the only human capable to put their gaze upon mine. There is earth witches that can sense us but not see us if we need a bargain for a spell."

It all seemed like a fantasy come true to her. But she knew that what he was saying was true with no lies in there in between, waiting to break free. Spring out into the midst.

There could not be any other option. Plus, he seemed incapable of lying.

"This is a lot to take in." She said truthfully with some confusion. "And Ruby? You dodged the question yet again." She knew there was more going on then what she could comprehend. His mind and learnings had hundreds of years on her mere human one.

His eyes came over more black and his expression darkened and became fierce. "My brother Rhys took her not long back. He mistook her for his own fated mate and so he took her off with him."

"He what!"

"The darkness that lingers in a part of the realm took him until it sucked him into its hold. He has always been in some part bad, that I knew, but I worry of poor Ruby who is nothing but endless good and pure light. Plus, I know and surely as you she is not into those like him. He could never be her mate in the way that he thinks."

The answer was simple to Elfina it did not require any soul searching, "Because she only likes woman." A statement and not a question.

"Oh, so you know?" He seemed surprised with that and ran a finger through her brunette hair. Hair with slight golden flecks and played with the ends of it, wrapping them around his fingers until they were firmly in his grip.

"Of course." Proudness of her sister flowed through her. But also, a fragment of worry.

"She also said to a woman that mistook her for competition that she preferred the cunt over cock!" He laughed as did she at that which took her by surprise that he could be so blunt. Then they looked at each other in a strange manner and both laughed again, making Elfina snort.

So, it was not just this pull, this blazing attraction that brought them together.

But someone else.

"I adore that girl so much." She looked at him inquisitively as he spoke. She could tell by his sad, defeated expression that her sister had gotten to him. She were glad though that her sister had not been alone in her death when she herself could not have been there.

It was their obvious caring of Ruby too. Their unconditional love for her. She had spent five years thinking that she were probably dead. But now... Excitement. Wonder.

She chuckled at his words. "That sounds just like Ruby. So, I can`t see her unless I become like you.... She is in danger then?" That stopped the laughter. Worry burned the back of her front.

To imagine that your sibling has been kidnapped by a psycho vampire, but oh yeah you are incapable of seeing them...

"No, not from my brother, if he believes she is his mate then she is safe as houses till he realises otherwise. He knocked me out somehow, It is fine though my precious one. You stay here and I will go across the realm to help her. I think I worked out that she can bring vampires to meet their fated mates and in that, that could be the danger that we fear for her." She did not reply but took his words in at once.

"No, no. I will come with you. Turn me. Then I can help get her back." She pleaded.

His eyes met hers and he gazed at her pleading face with awe. It was like he were thinking about it because he stared and stared at his mate as though he were taking in every inch of her and did not answer her immediately.

He did not mean to either.

"Iden. How does one become like you?" She enquired of him. Did he bite her and then she suddenly grew fangs?

"No." He said this and stood up, angrily shook his wings free, so they unfolded out of his back. She reached out to touch one, to feel it and to run a finger through it gently. Her eyes widened as she realised, they were harder then they looked but majestic still somehow.

A part of him, as though wings were a part of a bird. "You would have to die, that cannot be the plan for you right now. You have many more years left to live."

She put her hands upon her hips. "I am thirty years old, Iden. I am a fully grown woman I will have you know! I demand you turn me!"

"No!"

"Well then I will find someone who can." She turned as if to walk away to find someone.

"Yes, go on then." He yelled "Go off and find another vampire but I. Oh, but you can`t my one can you? Because you forget, they remain invisible to you and your people!"

"Argh!" She yelled annoyed at him and pushed him hard with all her curvy might. Ignoring the fact that a red car drove past, and she would yet again appear like a loon arguing with herself.

Typical!

Also marvelling at how his body was so hard as she pushed so it were almost like she were pushing lead. She felt aroused then at their simple but fiery arguing, even though she shouldn't do.

This annoying and stubborn vampire had got under her skin. And there she sensed there he would remain.

"I cannot believe that I am your fated mate. Hmm! I already feel like killing you now." She rolled her eyes and huffed. All he did were grin handsomely and to her horror he produced two almost flaming swords from behind his back. He passed them to her with ease.

"Here you go. Remember it's the head and nowhere else." He smiled mischievously. She did not go to touch them and therefore left them with him with a scowl.

"No. Enough games. Either you turn me now, or I am out of here. For good!"

She could sense him getting angry like a hidden power were unleashed. Not with her but with currents events. "It is not as simple as – oh I know let's turn you! You will be giving up being seen by everyone you know, and it is bloody horrible Elfina, for I myself have been there and it was- shit. You will have to leave here – this part of the planet - for good. I am the clan leader of part of the vampire realm, and I can't stay here forever. You would become eternal with me, yes, but you would be giving up motherhood, your job, friends, I know you don't have a family but if you did you would have to give that up too."

She thought for a moment. "Ruby is my family. You will be my family as well. Correct?"

"Always."

"I can do tattoos in the vampire realm can't I? The only thing is, is my dog. I want my dog with me. The dog or I stay human."

"Fair enough." He crinkled his nose. Obviously not a dog lover she gathered, but she knew in time that he would be once he met hers. If they were fated mates, there must be some common grounds there surely?

Because sex, attraction and desire was all good and well but eternal companionship... It needed more. Out of millions, billions they had been picked to be united together for life. There must be something there. Right? More.

And more she would bring.

He picked her up and she squealed and took her to a secluded spot that he knew off. Away from everyone. That was hard in a city! She could not go back home yet what with the police buzzing around her flat like flies on shit.

This that were about to happen - it needed privacy.

He appeared with her at the door of a large, mansion like house. Secluded away from everyone and located at the edge of the city. He knocked hard on the door.

"Where are we?" She whispered in confusion. But before he could answer, the door swung open and to her shock and horror there stood – no one! There was a sound, her ears took it in, but it was no words, no language that she knew of. More like static from a radio as Iden talked to whoever were at the door and she looked away uncomfortably. A whole new situation that she herself were not aware of.

"Can we seek shelter here?" Iden asked the shadow at the hidden door. He spoke for a little while whilst Elfina hung back cautiously and nervously.

It were a confusing situation to be fair. She could only see Iden, he and the house occupier could see everyone, and all humans would only see her!

It seemed like a yes, they could come in as the door swept open wide for them to enter. They were led through into the home by an invisible person, maybe multiple people, up the glorious winding stairs with thick cream carpet and into what was obviously a faraway guest room.

The door shut behind them with a slam.

"This is creepy." Elfina giggled unsurely and so sat on the large, cozy bed at the back of the huge room. She was worried about Sniggles, but she would be back for him if it were the last thing she did. She just had to trust her neighbour to watch him until she had done what needed to be done. Her loyal, four-legged friend would understand. He had to. They would be together again soon.

Iden nodded towards the door, "They are Martin and Claud. Old friends of mine that mainly live in the human realm but on special occasions they can be found at a mutual friend Barren`s. Don't worry he's a friend of mine also! Sometimes... Ruby adores him. They can be childish together when I cannot."

"I`ll bet. I remember what my sister were like. Silly. There is sure a lot to know." She sighed and gulped. He sat on the bed next to her and put an arm around her. She drew in his unworldly sense with her own. The scent that she guessed was made just for her. To entice her.

To keep her.

"And motherhood?" He asked gently. "If you are turned then there will be no little Elfina and Iden`s running around the place either mini human or vampires."

She shook her head. Her brunette hair flung out to the sides. Her lips moved as she spoke her truth, "It has never been my dream to have a house full of screaming children. If this were my friend Lovella, then there would be trouble from the start because she just loves kids, has always wanted to be a mum. God I am going to miss her! But me... I prefer animals myself. The peace that they bring. And I would prefer to be back with my sister then to be a mum. I would give it all up for her."

He side eyed her. "If that is your wish then I stand by that. You will have to die. Or be as close as you can possibly be. Martin and Claud have kindly gone out to give us time to... well you know...."

"To fuck?" her eyes blazed through his at the thought of it. Like the fire burned the same in her. In the way he burned for her. How he would do if it came down to it.

"No. To die. But we can do both if you like? If it would make it easier..." He said in all seriousness raising a brow.

Licking his lips in all earnest.

She smirked, trying to make a joke about the situation. "Well, I have always wanted to go out with a bang!"

And a bang she did.

He gently at first started to remove her clothes as she removed his. His old-fashioned ones.

Once they were both naked, he led her to the on suite where they gently showered. They both rubbed each other with the shower gel all over, soaping themselves up over and over. Once they were clean, he brought a plump breast to his mouth and roughly sucked it.

He bit into it with his fangs and left a bite on her breast that would soon unfortunately begin to heal. He flicked his tongue over her nipple over and over and took it into his mouth. She groaned in pleasure as he licked it.

The smell of her wetness, that any vamp could likely smell for miles, the evidence that she was enjoying it so very much.

She put her hand on his large, thick veined cock and without asking -wanked him off - hard. As she did this, enjoying hearing the vampire leader moan and thrust into her awaiting hand, he pushed his fingers deep into her cunt with no struggle.

There was no build up –no teasing- he went in straight for the kill. Vigorously pushing his fingers in and out of her much like he had done before but this time more wanting, until they both crashed and burned together with their endless bliss.

She glanced at the mirror, wanting to see them entwined together, all sudded up in the shower. But sadly, the rumours about vampires were in fact true – he had no reflection to speak of, all there were in the large full-length mirror, was her panting hard –and seemingly alone.

"You... you don't have a reflection!" He smirked not even bothered enough to look into the mirror to check that he did. "That is going to be a complete ass, not having a reflection when I want to do my hair after the change!" She said.

"You can see your own reflection, my vain little human mate." He laughed wickedly as if she were being a bit stupid with her question. "It is others that can`t see it." He laughed again. She loved the sound of his tinkering laugh; she could listen to the sound of his happiness all day long. Even if he were laughing at her.

She didn't mind. As long as she made him happy and made him groan.

His face went from a cold hearted serious one – to something else. Something – quite mesmerising.

"Oh, ok." She seemed confused like as if he had told her a riddle.

Now done but not quite, he led her boldly into the vacant bedroom and dried them off with some folded, clean white towels. Leaving a few drips that cascaded down her curvy body which he licked off of her as she moaned softly to his tongues reach.

He then grabbed her naked body and with his vamp speed he sped them both beside the wall, hooking her legs over his firm shoulder, lifting her up, he plunged his tongue right into her downwards centre and found the sweet full of nectar spot.

Having serviced many woman prior- both humans and then when he changed, only vamps, this would be the last one for him. He would rather burn to ash then lose that. It was all that he had pined for in all of his days.

All the envy he had felt at others meeting their fated mate now vanished as he licked her deep in her centre as though he could lick her for days.

He could quite honestly do that all day and never get tired of it because she tasted so darn sweet.

The teasing began as he licked, pulled away, kissed and sucked her mid centre and lapped up her wetness with a rather pro tongue. He groaned as she came hard on his face so suddenly that he hadn't read the signs.

"You can do that any time." He said wiping her sweet juice from his awaiting mouth. His fangs wanting to devour her, to feed the blood from near her crotch. She smelt and tasted so good down there to him, well everywhere that it hurt. His erection which had now sprung free was oozing with want and with need.

He placed her down gently onto the floor.

He looked her in the eye and said, "Suck me dry, human." She gasped at the blatant naughtiness of it all, but she wanted every ounce of it hidden away in her somewhere where she could not see it.

Almost purring in her delight at his big vampire cock, she gathered that this vamp, her mate, had the stamina of a top tier athlete.

Awesome!

He pushed her to the ground where she perched roughly on her knees, taking in his thick cock with her obvious eyes and wondering how it would actually fit into her small, pretty lipped mouth without suffocating her in any way.

What a way to go that would be! She could see the headlines now! Darn it!

But somehow, she knew that she would make it work. That cock had her name on it, stamped in invisible ink for only her to sense. She were hungry for it as if it were her last ever meal.

Which it kind of were because she were about to die...

Gulp.

"Lick it." He commanded and then groaned, tilting his head back as she with no hesitation took him firmly in with her mouth and throat until she could take it no more. It seemed like hours as she pleasured his cock until he cried as he filled her, until his seed dripped wantonly down her mouth and lips. Too much to fit in, too much to swallow.

"Naughty girl." Iden said huskily as he eyed his cum, wet on her stained lips. He did not care that his cum temporarily stained her mouth, instead he plunged his tongue deep inside of hers and their tongues merged roughly together in an all-powerful kiss.

She did not have a moment to think as he sped them both to the bed in the blink of an eye.

That was one move that she couldn't wait to try out when her blood no longer ran as a mortals.

"What now?" She asked him. Her eyes locked into his. Gasping with need, with want. Her nub and hidden area feeling both warm and used. Her hole wanting the cock that had just been down her throat.

"Now?" he said. "Now I will sadly have to kill you, my one."

There was a sharp pause and a sharp intake of breath as she took in his lingering words. Realising that she would have to meet her death at the hands of her soul mate in which she was fully aware would hurt him just as much as it would hurt her. To lose her humanity, her being seen by those that she adored, those she etched her ink on in her work.

Soon she would be all but invisible on the planet earth.

Would her dog even see her? That one hurt the most.

Soon her heart would beat no more but she would rise again – as his immortal mate.

CHAPTER TEN

I DEN
  He laid her down onto the bed as if she were made of glass or China and plunged his cock deep inside her. He tilted his head at her neck, and she nodded in consent at him feeding from there.

He sprung his fangs out into sharp points and stuck them right into her slender neck, making her gasp in surprise. He drank her down as she squirted her juices around his cock over and over at the sensations his cock brought as well as being eaten alive by his fangs at the same time.

She screamed in joyful pleasure which only turned him on even more and more. He did not think he could get any harder but he did.

He wanted to fill her up again, and again until his seed leaked out of her numb pussy.

He drunk and drunk until she murmured, "I feel light headed Iden." Her eyes rolled back in her skull.

She must know that she would be passing out soon and away from the land of the living.

Then she said something unexpecting- "Choke me, Iden. Do it right."

"What?" He frowned, unsure if he had heard her right. If he had, then it was an enticing offer indeed, one in which he would take great pleasure in doing as he fucked her.

"Choke me at the same time as draining me dry. Get it done quicker so we can spend all of eternity together." She whispered with a glow in her gaze.

The fear left her face and instead there was - peace.

She trusted this vamp. She wanted to be like him, to be with him, and to see her sister as many times as they both so wished. To see her and not just to hear her.

He nearly came right then as she whispered that. He nodded whilst drinking deep from her neck. Whilst still fucking her hard he pulled free from her slender neck and plunged his fangs into her wrist instead. With his right hand he squeezed her throat tightly, claw marks grazed her neck.

This was not how she envisioned her death.

She thought that she would maybe die peacefully in her sleep of old age, or in some kind of tragic accident in which everyone in her street mourned deeply for her, her funeral full to the brim with mourners. She did not think it would be caused by being fucked deep and hard by a vampire, her fated mate, whilst being strangled to death and bled dry of her blood at the same time.

But she was...surprisingly enjoying it. As she came hard and then so did, he, he increased the pressure onto her neck with his large hand and with that as he looked with passion into her eyes, never looking away until she at last passed out for good. He kept hold of her throat, wanting to let go so desperately with all of his might but knowing that he couldn't do so until he had squeezed all life out of her, so that she could be like him, one and the same, as the breath started to leave his stunning mate.

Looking like a queen with her brown hair splayed out, her pert lips puckered in wanting. Her eyes now sealed tight.

He pulled his cock free from her because it would be wrong to keep it in as she died and found one of his swords which he had laid on the cupboard in which he cut his wrist with it. As he bled his purple tinged blood, he made sure that it fell directly into Elfina's mouth which lay open, as it dropped into its target.

Time seemed to freeze.

He was eternal and had been around for many, many years, they flew bye at the speed of light.

But now as she lay still- it had frozen. For the next near seconds ahead were the most important ones of his life.

After five minutes or so of silence with him waiting, he began wondering. Had it worked? Had he done something wrong? Had he killed his one never to arise again?

Never stopping looking at her not even for a micro second, he got swiftly dressed and helped her into her clothes. Time were ticking and she had not risen at all. Had he killed his mate, strangled her only to be alone? If this were the case, then he would have to finally end himself. Just as he had tried to many moons ago when he were human.

For there would not be another but her.

He would have rather her stayed human, heck they could have worked it out somehow if they had tried! Sat down and talked, planned of how to be in love in two different realms. Being apart for many days would be preferable to never laying eyes on her again.

He could sense her life essence disappearing into thin air.

But then- her eyes flew startling open. Now a deep shade of crimson red, they were startling.

His darling, his mate. He expected her to shout, to order him around. But all she said as he laughed with eternal ever loving happiness at his newly turned baby vamp as her fangs protruded and her eyes yearned to go red was –

"Fuck, I'm hungry!"

CHAPTER ELEVEN

I DEN

"Oh my god it worked!" He swooped her into his massive arms and without being a good guest and saying goodbye to his hosts, to thank them if they were back from their journey, he opened a large bay window in the room they were currently in, and he shot them both straight to the judgement realm at quick speed.

There were no time to waste or no time to think. He wanted to show her his realm, his home that he were so proud of before she changed her mind and wanted to stay there in the human world.

Now both invisible to all humans they could do what the heck they liked while they were now on the way to her final judgement.

Even though she had the answer for she was finally one of the walking non breathers like he.

If she were not worn out, he could have thrust hard in to her dripping wet core as they flew along with his body pressed to hers. Now she were a vampire, he shuddered in pleasure at that, she would not be so fragile.

Not so – unbreakable.

But his.

"Where are we going?" She asked him sleepily in an odd lispy voice, as her new fangs scratched her mouth awkwardly. It would take a while to get used to speaking with fangs in her mouth. Getting used to drinking blood or if she were lucky – drinking it pure.

"To the judgement realm to sign you in my dearest mate. Then I am taking you to my home. Our home. Now." He grinned, his eyes lined with happiness and pride and nibbled her ear fruitily. Her whole entire scent was changing from that of a sweet dear human to a more tangy vampire stench.

Rotten to the core.

But as his mate, her scent was more delectable to him than any other would be. He could follow her anywhere and there would be no separation again.

Only eternal death.

He would behead any male that tried to separate them. Or female. Any prey was game when it involved keeping him from her. Or her from him.

His own brother included. He had let him off time and time again. For he was his brother and still of his blood. But if he touched his female then that would be the only reason for his brother to take a tumble.

A tumble into the never after.

"Where's my wings!?" She joked half-heartedly with a small frown as he gripped her tightly with both arms wrapped around her, never would he let her go.

Not now. Not ever. Obviously expecting that she would have been the one to fly them high through the day sky or side by side.

He sighed, "They are not ready yet, my one. Give them time for them to grow into something magnificent and then they will be yours forever." He kissed her forehead lovingly as they flew, and she grinned wildly as his lips met her cute head.

"It's quite exciting! But what about Sniggles?"

"The mangy mutt will be fine darling. We will get him once you have settled in."

"Please."

Not long later she noticed the sky was changing from a light baby blue into – she did not know what, but it became blurry as though there was something else approaching them. The air sizzled like electric and then they to her amazement they were now instead of soaring through the sky – firmly on the ground!

He put her down carefully and she stumbled along after him. When she stopped to look around the small place where they were now, he grabbed her hand and held it tightly.

"Now Elfina. These that work here are very important people. So please do not try to eat them. Ok? Also, if you see anyone else that tempts you to take a bite – don't. just don't. Even though you are a baby vamp, full of thirst and want, you are still expected to show some decorum in there. These souls are here to be judged and not to be bled dry."

"I understand." He noticed her lick her lips as he mentioned bleeding dry and was now a bit wary of taking his new vampire mate straight into the lion's den. Heck as long as she remained calm, and they didn't get Victor then it should be all good!

"The judgers are all...dwarfs. Try not to offend them in any way and you should be fine my mate." He tapped her on the shoulder. This felt rather hypocritical as Iden knew that he often unintentionally, sometimes intentionally offended people. But he could defend himself, she needed to rest and to gain her strength so her wings could spread.

They reached a large building, and she followed him meekly as they entered it. Her mouth drooling causing her to look embarrassed.

He took her through the large entrance, through to the main room. White as white can be there was no other colour.

"It's a bit white..." She whispered. All the judgers eyes shot round to look at who dared insult their stunning décor.

"What colour would you go for? Pink?" A dwarf man with red curly hair like Ronald McDonald glared at Elfina who he evidentially felt had disrespected them all in her first time there.

"Careful mate." Iden hissed at the dwarf. Ready to go into battle for his soon to be bride – and win.

"As you are a newbie, I will let you off..."

"Sorry I was not trying to offend. It is lovely here. Really lovely." Elfina apologised with her hands out. Knowing that as Iden had explained before that she would be soul collecting or something. So, she rightfully assumed that should be here in this building often. She needed to bond with these people. Angels, whatever they were.

She pulled back and cringed as she then noticed the ghost like souls in the room ready for judging. A tall, skinny guy with a sneer and a hooked nose, who was in disbelief that he were dead and shouting at everyone with a string of cusses on awakening to a bright room full of small people .

For such small people and see through souls, the room were lively.

Frankly she loved it already! Was this her home? She vaguely remembered Iden telling her about another realm that were out there, so she guessed not. Her mate lovingly poked her out of her daydream and guided her towards the next available seat with a gentle tug.

Even though she were in a trance like state still she flushed at his mere touch. Her vamp newness flowing through her and making her feel...horny for Iden. Even his gentle touch raised her senses. His grip she longed to feel elsewhere. Did this happen to all vampires?

"Stop touching me." She said quietly and pulled away as the invisible sparks flew.

"Why?"

"Its... intense." She blushed with red cheeks flushed red. "I feel... everything."

Iden frowned and looked at her with a frown. "Why?"

"The touch. It`s intense..."

It then dawned on him what she really meant. For it had been so long since he himself had turned. He remembered the blood thirst but had forgotten the senses being flooded. Increasing the touch, smell, feel and... taste....

"No problem." He let her go after a quick brush of the arm. She groaned and he smirked. She scowled. Clearly irritated with him so he winked at her to wind her up yet more.

The next eternity was going to be fun!

"Hi, I'm Victor." A short man with glasses interrupted the love birds, as he ran over to Elfina who were twiddling her thumbs nervously, "No need to worry lovey, let`s get you settled in. I see you have a body as well as a soul so I'm guessing a new vamp? That is good we need more collectors now the humans are going through an obesity crisis..." He laughed at his poor joke as he clearly knew what she was just by her looks alone.

The only new ones that walked through that realm with a body were newly made vampires. Everyone else that arrived were merely souls. Their bodies left to be buried on earth. "Where's your turner?"

Victor turned his head around and let out a sigh.

"Here I am!" Iden waved mockingly.

"Oh. You." Victor looked almost like someone had kidnapped his only puppy.

"You know each other?" Elfina looked from the scowling glasses wearing dwarf to the tall brooding vamp and back again. Sensing the tension running there between the two males that encased the room.

"Nope never seen him before!" Iden said awkwardly.

"You liar!" Victor turned her way. " You have to watch this one mam he is a nightmare. I have some questions that I am just going to quickly type up after all time is..."

"Short," Finished Iden.

"Right, you are for a change. So Lovely lady." Iden growled and Victor shot him a look back. "Reason for turning?"

"He is my fated mate." Elfina explained. Looking at her vampire mate with a swoon.

"Oh. You lucky, lucky thing." The short judge said with a strong hint of sarcasm behind his words that no one in the room would be able to miss.

"She is." Idem beamed, ignoring the slur to his character.

"Cause of death?" As this was asked, Elfina didn't speak as though she didn't know what to say. "I said cause of death?" Victor probed.

She did not answer and lowered her head as though shamed.

"Jeez. Time is short you need to know that if you want to work here eternally! Let's hope your soul collecting is better and quicker than your speaking." Said Victor quietly.

Knowing that vampires had enhanced hearing and as a baby vamp hers would be extra sharp but going for gold anyway. Elfina gulped.

She had only cared about Ruby, to think long term about what was ahead. But it was too late to do anything about it for now she were stuck.

For she was dead. And an eternal blood drinker with that.

"I strangled her."

"You. Strangled her. You killed your mate?" The small man was lost for words. He eyed Elfina and then glanced at Iden then back again.

Elfina were surprised that he didn't have whiplash.

"That is correct. Her name is Elfina, she is my fated mate. Now I know I have already had a few days off, but I am now on a serious mission to rescue another vampire and so I will need some time off from collecting."

The judge nodded, "You have a week Iden, two tops. But if you are needed before the mission is done then this mission will have to cease at once. Got it?" He peered through his glasses. "The only reason I am allowing it is you have a baby vamp mate that you need to keep control of, and she will need to recover before her collection can at first begin."

"And wings." Added Elfina. Stroking a finger down her own back and feeling nothing growing as of yet. She had imagined that they would spring out in an instant. But alas she had been wrong.

"And wings." Parroted Victor. "Won't be long, I'm sure. Also, Iden although you are the biggest arsehole I have ever met, and I have met many, you have always done your share of collecting plus much more if so required. So go on take the time off, and good luck with your mission. Now Elfina this lady here will take you for a finger print and a quick scan and you can go on your way. It's all relatively straight forward."

Victor gestured at a plump lady with hazel eyes and who liked to be of Chinese origins. She got up and went to follow the short lady who smiled shyly at Victor as though she had a sweet and innocent crush.

"I think she likes you." Iden said.

"I should hope so, she is my wife of many, many years. This is my Bibby Ray." Gesturing at his wife.

"Hello." She said nicely to Elfina, grimacing at Iden as though he was the plague itself come back to kill them all.

Iden turned towards her geeky husband. "I didn't know you were married?" He said this politely whilst looking to the door out of boredom.

Victor studied the taller male for a moment with distrust, "That is because you are the type not to get to know people. Me and Bibby have been together over eight hundred years. Some of the best years of my life! I have known you even longer and you still forget my name on the daily, or else you pretend not to know it..."

Iden was not listening again to the man's gormless waffling and was instead watching his mate being led over to the scanner. She looked thirsty and he knew they would have to hurry and get her, her first blood before she came undone.

Now were the time that she – and everyone else were at the most vulnerable to her change.

The beacon did not holler or glow red as Elfina touched the pad, but her mate knew it wouldn't. It did not matter if it did, she belonged to him and the vampire realm now, and her soul was forever linked to his so she could not be dragged to the lower realms kicking and screaming by one of the lizard like freakish creatures that walked the lower realms, punishing the torturous souls forever.

To be her mate as well as her sire entwined them twice over. Nothing could break them.

All they needed now was to rescue Ruby from his deranged brother and to not get pulled into the darkness, get most of her essential things from her flat and her musty, crusty dog from the batty old lady that offered to watch him.

Then they could settle into new vamp life.

Show her to his people proudly. Soar to the earth together to bring the dead on their journey.

"Hey! Careful!" Iden came out of his whirling thoughts as he noticed that one of the dwarfs -a blonde female had cut themselves somehow. With her new vamp speed, Elfina sped over to the unsuspecting woman, knocking past little Bibby and grabbing hold of the woman with hunger.

Her nails turned into claws and her perfect pale face become – deadly, but still like a dream for his mate. To see her as her vampire form for the first time was something else entirely.

He wanted her so bad.

To fuck as the undead without a hint of a pulse throbbing between them. But he had to protect her. If she fucked up now, then she could be banished for all time- on day one of her new identity.

Her identity as a vampire. The clan leader`s queen.

Luckily Iden was quicker then she as she let out a scary shrieking growl, her eyes as she were hungry grew blacker then black as though she had no pupils at all, "Elfina!"

He pulled her to him fast and as there were cries to take her out of there at once, he swooped her up and took her out of there just like were suggested.

Or ordered. She was for the moment as strong – possibly stronger then him right then and it were a struggle to get her out of the room without her taking a bite out of the blonde judge who had scattered off in her panicked alarm. The scent of her blood now merged with the hint of his mates stress sent Iden over the edge.

Nearly wanting to step back into the building and feast on the small blondes blood himself - with his mate at his side. To bite all the judgers until it were only souls left in there.

"I`m hungry Iden. So hungry." She moaned in frustration from losing her dinner.

"Let's go home my love." He simply said.

"I would like that. Is there food of the liquid kind?"

Meaning blood. Oh.

He chuckled at her insatiable hunger as he gripped her tightly in his love hold and he took her home. "Well, about that..." He said lightly to her. Remembering that he had been on a blood vial drinking spree prior to going looking for his mate and so sadly all available stocks at his large home were then currently left dry.

Much like Ashley nicking all his alcohol.

Knowing that he would have to call on his friends, his clan, or others, anyone really that had no heart beat to speak of to get the much-needed blood to his door pronto.

After all he had a hungry new vampire mate to feed...

EPILOGUE 1

ELFINA
They had entered the vampire realm in a short of amount of time as was actually doable. Iden was not sure that his dark wings were still in one piece after the flight there, for he had never flown that fast in his many years of existence.

Nor did he want to ever again after that.

Elfina looked around with stars blazing in her eyes at what she could now see, what she could feel. What she wanted to touch. Her temporary arousal was gone as there was only one thing going through her mind.

Because there was a hungry felling in the pit of her tummy somewhere, much like when she had been and hit it hard on the town and the next day, she went and got a bad case of the munchies. Not this time she wasn't craving her favourite cheesy quavers or even a bacon sandwich with a dob of ketchup - but blood.

Human blood. Or otherworld one would do.

That judge when she had cut herself back in the judgement realm had smelt so darn good that she had felt herself drool with hunger at the sight of it as it dripped from the small woman's skin.

When the scent had lingered on, she had sped off towards the dwarf before her brain had even ordered herself too!

The realm she were now in was eerie as it just looked like being back home on the human world. But instead of houses of all kinds it was mansions everywhere, exquisite old ones that would have cost a fortune on earth.

Like something from roman times.

Old as dust. The vamps clearly liked good things in life for that she could see! She only knew what Iden had told her about it all but now she could see for herself. This was now her forever home where she would spend all of eternity.

A week ago, this whole realm before her would have been hidden from her gaze as it were others, but now – now she could see everything that it so possessed! That this was the main realm, but it also contained vast oceans, forests and beaches a few miles away for one to sunbathe on.

Instead of shops there they had large stores. Because no one had to work if they so chose, except to soul collect.

Everything that she could possibly dream of ever wanting or ever needing in exchange for an eternity of soul collecting.

Except for blood there of course which in her view was... odd. After all wasn't that the most important thing that vampires needed to get by?

To live even.

Silly really that it wasn't available on tap. She wondered who at first had created the vamps and why they got them working without the liquid they needed to survive?

As they traipsed together through his clans main part of the realm, she looked and smiled nervously at all the many curious vamps that peered out of their huge houses straining to see her, and who loitered in the streets to look at the newbie vamp with mere, sudden interest.

One of the fated ones.

It was like being at the theatre but she herself was on the stage and not in the audience.

While Iden went off and left her for a brief moment to speak to some nearby realm occupiers as she had nicknamed then already, she stood and gripped a hold of her own wrist and felt for a pulse. Knowing that she was now on of the dead but also still feeling... feeling that it was still hard to imagine it.

Nothing were there though. She put a hand on her plump chest and listened for the usual thud thud of her heart, that had kept her alive each and every day for thirty strange years.

No heartbeat. Check again. Still none.

She held her breath in knowing that she would not die from the lack of air in her body- for she were now clearly dead already. It was so, so weird that she found it difficult to comprehend or to imagine in any way. She could not hold it in for too long because if felt – simply wrong.

She exhaled.

Thirty years of breathing in and out every day would do that to someone.

"Odd, isn't it?" A soothing masculine voice from behind her caused her to spin round nervously to greet them. She looked and behind her was a dark-haired god like man. Thinner and not as bulkier as her own mate but with a mischievous glint in his eyes that showed he were probably, hopefully harmless.

As harmless as a blood sucking, fanged vampire could be anyway...

Almost as stunning as Iden himself, her Iden were.

She studied the handsome stranger and giggled as he must have seen her checking her own bloody pulse and heartbeat, to check them, to check her, "Yes. Yes, it is!"

"I have not breathed for hundreds of years at least, and it still is odd even to myself that we are this way." The man said in all honesty.

She were glad that she were not the only one to feel that and that he spoke truthfully without keeping it from her, "Elfina." She held out a shaking hand to his large one.

"Barren." He grinned and passed her his own one whilst cautiously looking around to make sure Iden didn't come running over to them like a bear with a sore head at him daring to touch his mate.

For all with a brain knew that all vampires were territorial over their mates.

Especially newly mates ones like these two were

"I know this is forward of me, but I don't suppose...." She asked of him and lowered her gaze.

"You want blood." He paused and eyed her. "Yes, I do lass I am just waiting for Iden to return because..." He looked at her as if he did not want any trouble from her. As if that man could be over powered by little old her.

Clearly unaware of the power she now held as a newly bitten one...she could probably push him over with just a single finger!

"Give me it. Please!" Her eyes changed colour, darker, and her fangs bit into her mouth again and she tasted her own purple liquid that now spilled into her mouth. She knew as a baby vamp that it would take a while for her to be able to control herself somewhat and to not keep biting her own mouth and tongue when her fangs burst out for a bite.

But this was...becoming embarrassing.

Begging a stranger for some blood as if she were begging for cock from a hottie. If she was not mated, then she would probably have offered herself to him just to get her first taste of pure liquid pleasure that she so desperately wanted to gorge on.

"Please!" louder that time.

"I..."

Iden saw the commotion that had started to build and raced over in seconds. Knocking past someone roughly as he sped over but not even caring or stopping to say sorry.

"Hey!" The man cried out annoyed.

He ignored them.

His mate was his priority for now, "Come, my Elfina." He glowered at Barren who glowered back in turn at him. Leading her at once towards the house before she became unstable due to her unbearable hunger that would start to eat away at her until she fed it.

Barren traipsed along slowly behind them both and was soon followed by Ashley who was as usual drinking new whisky straight from the bottle. His two most trusted friends if he had to use that term lightly seeing in his new mate.

Iden used his own powers to open the door of the massive house, his home, and they all went inside.

Before he had, had time to offer her a seat, "I`m hungry Iden." She pleaded again to him in a sexy voice to him with a sexy whine behind it. To hungry to think to take in the superiority of the home that would soon be Her's also.

Christ on a bike, Iden had forgotten how thirsty newbies were for the red stuff! It seemed as though she would trade her left arm over it! Or even her left nipple!

"Barren? The blood if you may." Iden said. Once it was received by him, he cautiously handed her the large bottle of blood, for desperate times called for desperate measures and so they all stood and waited for a reaction to her first taste of the good stuff.

They needed to see how she was after drinking it for the first time as that were the danger period for all new vamps.

Her sister, Iden had noted had been like a pro after her first red meal. She had been on edge for a short time as was usual but not as on edge as some that he had seen in all his days.

Some newbies were so hunger filled that it was all they thought about for the first few months that they could think of no other and they could not soul collect until they had settled down.

She sniffed it in enjoyment and then drunk it quickly down. It was no more the rusty tasting liquid that she herself had caught a taste of as a human accidentally. Now it were – like heaven itself had been put into a bottle just for her.

She groaned in ecstasy making her mate hard once again.

"Mmm." She licked her lips with her tongue as the last of the blood went down her throat with a trickle. She gasped at the new power that she felt coursing inside her. More, she wanted more damn it! Damn them, damn everybody!

She clenched her small fists as though she was about to begin a fight with all that were watching her in the room.

"Bloody hell mate." Ashley fanned himself with a hand at the heat in the room. "I hope my own mate is just as ravenous with her meals. Amongst other things..." he grinned at his leader.

Iden grinned back, "Oh yes, she is ravenous ok. For me and my big..."

"Iden! I am still here you know!" Elfina said. He did not apologise but instead winked. "Whose this?" She eyed Ashley warily. "Do you have more blood for me?"

"No, I'm afraid I don't. And I'm Ashley." He smiled as he chugged whisky down in the same way she had just chugged the blood down.

"Oh. Does that help with the cravings then?" She pointed at Ashley's bottle with a lone finger. She would try anything, anything at all to not want the blood so badly. She had just had a load after all and still pined for more!

"Yes, to be honest, it does. I could rip someone's face off without it." Ashley said in all honesty. "Else I need a lot of blood to satisfy me."

"I never knew that." Iden said glancing in astonishment at one of his oldest friends. Why did he not know of this? He just assumed that his dark-skinned, cheeky friend had a drink problem all these years that they had been acquainted but it had been something else.

"Nope, me neither." Admitted Barren also with an embarrassed shrug.

"Why didn't you say something? All those times that I told you off for drinking my stocks of alcohol dry. I wouldn't have minded so much... if I knew."

"Eh, it was nothing. But yes, going back to the question, Elfina was it? It does."

Iden reached over and brushed a comforting hand on his friends shoulder. "Now I feel bad for calling you a pisshead all these years."

"Hey, It does not matter. We know you as all mighty grumpy twat."

Iden looked at his friends not quite knowing if Ash was serious or playing with him about the nickname.

"What's mine?" Asked Barren curiously.

"Posh totty." Ashley said with a smirk.

"Fair play."

Elfina began trembling with need as she shook all over and so Iden pulled out a chair and sat her down gently into it. She growled and mewed like an angry kitten at his touch but then smiled in apology.

Iden had an important task for his dear companions, "Now guys. I have to leave for the darkness. Could you watch Elfina for me? I also have to go get her stinky ass dog so could you watch that as well? Ash you can be temporary leader. Barren you are temporary second in command. If I don't come back... Look after her for me. Please, with your life. And obviously keep those titles in the event of my actual death.

"Kinda, wishing you don't come back then." Ashley joked. But then his faced dropped and he eyed his clan leader seriously and put the whisky down on the side cupboard with a clang. "No mate. Please take care of yourself. We will be honoured to look after your mate for you. It is a privilege to be asked. Is the dog friendly?"

"Thank you, my friend. And yes, yes, it is. I think."

"Thank you but I am going with him." Elfina said shakily.

Iden was used to stubborn woman in his life so without fail he would make her see sense, "No, my mate you are staying here with Ash and Barren. I will be fine on my own and Ruby will come back with me safe and sound. You will see her soon." He kissed her on the head.

Ashley sighed, "Unless your brother kills you first, my friend."

This was a possibility.

"Let him try." Iden grew dark with spiralling rage. Not even his own flesh and blood could keep him from achieving his goals. He should have pulled his brother free from the darkness when he had the chance.

He grew monstrous.

"No one is killing anyone, well us anyway. I know he is your brother, but I swear to god. Wait... is god real?" Elfina asked with a curious tilt of the head. She still had so much to learn from the realm and everything ese but now she had an eternity to learn it in.

"We aren't sure either to be honest." Iden shrugged. "We all think so as there is a higher master somewhere that commands the judgers. It is a mystery to us as it is to you, my one."

Iden did not like admitting to his mate that there was somethings that even he did not know for fear of looking stupid to her.

But they didn't know. Nobody did or if they did, they had kept shtum all these years.

Elfina thought for a moment, "Weird. Ok I swear to god if he exists that I know he is your brother but if he lays one single finger on you or hurts one hair on your pretty chiselled face..."

Iden beamed at that and did not try to hide it.

"Then I will... but anyway I am coming with you so I will see for myself!" Her eyes grew black at the thought of her mate being harmed in anyway. She shakily got up from the chair, sped over to him, and held him in a tight, possessive grip with her own.

"Well then." Iden turned around and spoke to the room with Elfina hanging tight to him like a limpet. "This shall be fun. Me and my beautiful fated one here, who is currently likely blood starved, on edge, and likely to kill everyone and anyone that pisses her off in any way, shape or form, will go with myself to rescue dear Ruby. This could become a bit of a shit show believe me and the darkness could swallow us whole never to be seen again. Or Rhys could go nuclear again and end us. So, we will grab the mangy dog for you to watch for us if you please, and then we will be on our way in the morning at suns first light."

"As I said before. Take care my friend."

"Please bring little Ruby back. We still haven't been to see that film we were going to see together yet!" Barren joked. Iden scowled. Fucking Mario.

And with that two of the friends made themselves comfortable in the humungous house of their grumpy ass leader, while Iden and Elfina got ready to visit the darkness.

Before the darkness visited them all.

EPILOGUE 2

R^{HYS}
The next morning once Sniggles was back in his owners reach, Iden and Elfina trundled through towards the darkness aimlessly, Iden taking the lead and Elfina struggling to keep up what with being a newly developing vamp, the oh so dark one- Rhys sat on a makeshift throne in his glorious castle. Surrounded by fire and blazing lava, his castle was in front of a volcano.

Trendy.

Dragons flew high in the dark swirly air and crazed unicorns shrieked in what were left off the trees that were there. Nothing was nice there. But still some wanted to stay. Some wanted the thrill of bad rather than the quenching release of doing good for another.

The sunshine was gone in the sky – replaced with something else entirely...

"They are coming for me." Ruby said with a scowl to the tall, dark horrible vamp that sat upright on his throne with no slump to his person. She wore a black, stunning dress that she had been made to wear that she hated more than this guy that had imprisoned her there. It matched his black suit and trainers.

Luckily for her he had not touched her in any way since he had first tried on her first day there, as she did not think she would be able to handle a guy touching her like that again after her disgusting attack from five years ago.

It made her stomach crawl to think of being penetrated, even just touched, and she guessed that Rhys was fully aware of that for he had not tried since. And he seemed the sort that was a bit of a goer from all the sexual innuendo jokes he made.

Not funny ones.

"I know." Rhys grinned evilly with a twist of thin lips. He was so darn bad, Ruby thought that if he smiled with happiness even now and again that he could look somewhat handsome to some. But the whole bad thing, bad boy act he had going on with trying too hard to be bad all the time was dragging his looks down in her simple opinion.

Her neutral one.

"You must know by now that I am not, she who you have been searching for." She explained quietly. Meaning his oh fated one that she really wasn`t.

He eyed her with a roll of the dark soulless eyes. "I...I am beginning to see that now my pretty. But why did you smell of her then back when?" His dark eyes with a trace of red burned deep into hers at the remembrance of the delicious smell that had invaded his senses a few days prior when he had busted in on his brother.

And found oh so much more.

He flexed his clawed fingers, and she sighed in annoyance and possibly boredom with that. Because they had been over and over the same thing like a stuck record since she had been brought there and kept prisoner by his great, dark lordship.

And sometimes her head fogged over, and her thoughts became...dark. She could only guess what the darkness had done to this vicious man in front of her over the years was what it were trying to do to her.

Many people would have gone mad, unhinged, with the insanity of it all! But she was now strong. Strong as come be.

She had, had to have been.

"I don't know." She muttered quietly.

For she did not. And she was beginning to worry that she would be penalised for not doing her work, although this male there had said he had temporarily sorted it with the judgers.

Had he though?

He could find his mate and live evilly ever after, and she could be banished or put down even for not doing her soul work in her absence. Which was a bit difficult when she was locked in some eerie fucking castle and only given blood every now and again when he remembered that she was also a blood sucker like him!

Rhys growled, "Well then you will be here for a long time my pretty. Let's hope the darkness doesn't take you before my brother tries to." He winked.

But to him the darkness was great. He did not see everyone's problem with it. If he could have his own way the whole realm would be shrouded in it.

"He will kill you before that happens! He and my sister. His mate." Ruby said. She gasped in realisation as Rhys spun round in a fierce whirlwind. The shadows that often lingered in the room followed him everywhere that he went now as if he was their daddy.

Did they follow him out of the realm she had wondered, or did they stay in there impatiently waiting for him?

Rhys held his chin and thought like the villain he were, "His mate? Hmm. That is new. I wonder what she is like, this here mate?" Rhys walked to a large window and looked out at the fiery surroundings that he adored.

Black crows hollered noisily outside. He put his hands together and a ball of light flew out and held in his palm. He muttered some words of forbidden to them dark magic, and then looked into the magnificent light, and he could see his only brother and his weary new blood mate had just stepped through his part of the realm from theirs.

The power of the dark could only show him that area or else he would have used it to find... her.

His own one.

When the lass he had captured had said she was not into guys back then he had just assumed she were playing hard to get with him at first until she had flinched and appeared frightened under his not so gentle first touch. But now it was obvious she were telling the truth about who she truly were. Because woman all around fawned after him and his good looks and his –undiluted power.

"Let him try my dear. Let him try." He scoffed. "Fess where are you; you fool!" He hollered.

And with that he left the room in a flustering hurry and slammed the door hard too. And the shadows followed adoringly behind him...

The end for now.
        Until Rhys`s book...

Don't miss out!

Visit the website below and you can sign up to receive emails whenever Tanya Coleby publishes a new book. There's no charge and no obligation.

https://books2read.com/r/B-A-FMUS-ZVYJC

BOOKS 2 READ

Connecting independent readers to independent writers.

Also by Tanya Coleby

His Invisible Hold
His Invisible Hold

The Fable Gems
Flashbacks
Abduction

The human sensor series.
The Human Sensor
The Human Sensor
The Human Sensor 2

Standalone
His Hope Her Wolf

Ingram Content Group UK Ltd.
Milton Keynes UK
UKHW010851130723
425071UK00001B/55